RED VELVET
AND ABSINTHE

WITHDRAWN

RED VELVET
AND ABSINTHE

PARANORMAL
EROTIC ROMANCE

EDITED BY
MITZI SZERETO

FOREWORD BY
KELLEY ARMSTRONG

CLEiS
PRESS

Published in the United States by Cleis Press, Inc., 2246 Sixth Street, Berkeley, California 94710.

Printed in the United States.
Cover design: Scott Idleman/Blink
Cover photograph: Rekha Garton/Getty Images
Text design: Frank Wiedemann

First Edition.
10 9 8 7 6 5 4 3 2 1

Trade paper ISBN: 978-1-57344-716-4
Ebook ISBN: 978-1-57344-738-6

Contents

For the moon never beams without bringing me dreams...

—"Annabel Lee," Edgar Allan Poe

FOREWORD

The tradition of Gothic literature stretches back to the early days of the novel, with Horace Walpole's *The Castle of Otranto*, published in 1764. Anyone who has read Poe or Stoker or Daphne du Maurier would recognize the early gothic elements in Walpole's story. The story begins with a tragedy—a lord's son dies on his wedding day. The lord then decides to marry the girl himself. She flees to a church. The lord pursues and is about to kill her rescuer when a birthmark reveals that the young man is his own son. The lord locks him in a tower, but he escapes with the girl into the catacombs. And so it continues, a melodramatic tale of murder, betrayal and mistaken identity, with a bittersweet romantic ending. By the third edition, the book's subtitle had changed from "A Story" to "A Gothic Story." And so a genre was launched.

Classic Gothic literature, with its stock elements—innocent heroine, mysterious hero, isolated setting, curses, madness, secrets—has gone in and out of fashion since Walpole. In the sixties and seventies, it saw a revival with Gothic romantic suspense, most notably in the books of Victoria Holt, Barbara Michaels and Mary Stewart. These novels often included an element of the supernatural, but it was usually subdued. A ghost might hold the key to a secret or a character might discover her ancestors were witches. The erotic elements were even more subdued. Rarely was there anything more explicit than kisses and longing. Even the erotic subtext was muted, far more than it had been in Gothic novels written a century earlier.

In the late seventies, Gothic fiction began another turn, one that firmly embraced both the sensual and the supernatural. Leading this new era was Anne Rice, who returned to the early days of the genre, following in the footsteps of Bram Stoker and James Malcolm Rymer by putting vampires at the center of her work. Her sensual vampires were not the monsters, though, but the protagonists. Twenty-five years later, authors took Rice's ideas even further, and the genre of paranormal romance was born, replete with sexy supernaturals of every variety, from vampires and werewolves to angels and demons. And these were not the chaste encounters seen in the Gothic romances of the sixties. These were erotic, often explicitly so, exploring every facet of sexuality from GLBT to poly relationships to S/M to fetish.

Red Velvet and Absinthe celebrates the Gothic in all its forms and adds in the erotic elements that were often glossed over in the genre's early incarnations. Here we do find traditional historical tales and exotic settings, but we'll also find contemporary stories, and those with a magical surrealism that transcends time. The stock elements are well represented, too, often with an original twist, giving us delicious tales of family secrets and horrible curses, enchanted paintings and mysterious beverages.

Those looking for the supernatural will not be disappointed. Stories feature not only recognizable creatures, such as werewolves and ghosts, but mysterious ones too, men whispered to be demons or golems, and new fantastical beasts born from the authors' imaginations.

Whatever the setting or the time period or the elements chosen, all these stories embrace the emotional and sensory richness integral to the Gothic tale. We don't just read words on a page. We feel the red velvet. We taste the absinthe. We smell the flower and sweat. We hear the whispers and cries. And we experience the thrilling danger, the looming apprehension, the exquisite passion. That is the core of Gothic literature and this collection delivers.

Kelley Armstrong

INTRODUCTION

The genre of paranormal romance has had a very respectable history, having taken shape from the Gothic novel, which falls solidly into the category of Romantic literature. To the uninitiated, this might seem a bit odd, considering that Gothic literature is most often associated with elements we might not consider particularly romantic or sexy. I don't know many people who'd consider howls in the night, creaking staircases, rattling chains, and a madwoman locked in the attic the stuff of romance. But those of us readers who have enjoyed a long-term love affair with Gothic fiction can wholeheartedly attest to the fact that there is, indeed, a romantic theme running through these works, even in the darkest and grimmest of offerings. So too, are there elements of sensuality and eroticism. Anyone who's read Bram Stoker's *Dracula* will tell you that eroticism is alive and well on the pages. The impassioned torment taking place between Heathcliff and Catherine in Emily Brontë's classic *Wuthering Heights* provides some steam as well, even if not overtly expressed in the prose.

Perhaps it's that delicious shiver we feel running down our spines when we read these works that keeps us coming back for more. Perhaps it's that subtle sense of fear that thrills us and gives us a forbidden charge that's ever so slightly erotic in nature. Whatever it is, Gothic literature is as popular now as it was in the past. Although the greats such as Bram Stoker, the Brontë sisters, Mary Shelley and Daphne du Maurier are long dead, we have a host of contemporary authors keeping the Gothic spirit alive and interpreting it in new and exciting ways. It is these writers past and present to whom I owe a debt of gratitude—both as a reader *and* as a writer.

Red Velvet and Absinthe is a book I've wanted to do for a long time. Having enjoyed Gothic novels since childhood, it was inevitable I'd one day wish to do something along these lines myself. The fact that the paranormal has been experiencing an even further renaissance beyond the written word thanks to the recent output from the film and television industries finally gave me the impetus. My goal for *Red Velvet and Absinthe* was to offer readers a collection of unique and original stories that conjure up the rich atmospheric and romantic spirit of the Gothic masters (and mistresses), but take things further by adding to the brew a generous portion of eroticism that's far less restrained than what transpired between Cathy and Heathcliff. I hope this will be a collection our literary predecessors would have enjoyed reading, had any of them been alive to witness its publication.

So I'd like to invite you to lie back and relax and listen to the wind howling outside your window as you read these stories in the flickering light of a candle, the absinthe you're sipping warming your body like the caressing touch of a lover's fingers....

Mitzi Szereto
(Writing from a windswept moor somewhere in England)

SNOWLIGHT, MOONLIGHT

Rose de Fer

She remembered the snow; the snow and the blood and the velvet night. She had lain gazing up at the icy indifferent moon as her strength slowly ebbed and at last the darkness claimed her. That was when she'd heard them start to sing. The wolves: the terrible, beautiful wolves.

The full weight of the night pressed itself down on her but beneath her there was only softness, comfort. She couldn't move, couldn't even open her eyes. From far away she heard music. A piano, deep and resonant, soothing.

She felt calm. No, that wasn't quite true. She felt as though she was *meant* to feel calm. As though she was somehow disconnected from whatever lay on the other side of the darkness. As though she'd been drugged.

With great effort she finally managed to curl the fingers of her right hand, slowly breaking the spell that held her immobile. Her skin began to tingle with awareness. It seemed like years before she got the fingers to open again, and by then the tingling had begun to spread with nearly unbearable pleasure throughout her body. Tears pricked her eyes beneath the lids and her heart swelled with euphoria as the melody reached a climax. Was this death?

She reached out in the darkness, feeling for the snow. Instead her hand encountered a hard unyielding surface and something crashed to the floor. The music stopped abruptly and a crescendo of sharp taps told her someone was coming.

At last she managed to open her eyes and the room swam into being. She lifted her head and took in her surroundings. She was lying in a four-poster bed hung with heavy damask curtains that were tied back with braided cords. A fire roared in the hearth opposite the bed, and the room was lavishly decorated.

A man stood over her, his blue eyes dancing in the light of the candle he placed on the bed table. He was elegantly dressed in a black frock coat and matching silk cravat. A gold watch chain hung across the front of his burgundy waistcoat.

"You're awake at last," he said, in a soft cultured voice.

"At last?"

"You've been asleep for some time. Do you remember anything?"

She searched her mind. The forest. The moon. "The carriage," she said suddenly. "It overturned!"

"Yes. You had crawled some distance off the road into the trees. When I found you, you were nearly dead. I'm afraid there was nothing I could do for your coachman."

"And you brought me here?"

He nodded. "I patched you up and let you sleep."

"Patched me up?" Frightened, she raised her arms and gasped in horror at what she saw. The skin was crisscrossed with jagged wounds that had been expertly stitched together with black thread. Her hand fluttered to her throat where she could feel the evidence of an even worse injury—clearly a near-fatal one. Her eyes brimmed with tears. "Dear god, what happened to me?"

"It was rather a nasty accident, I'm afraid. Still, you're over the worst of it now. And no matter the unfortunate circumstances, I'm honored to have you as my guest, Miss...?"

She opened her mouth to tell him her name, then frowned in confusion. "That's strange. I can't seem to remember."

He smiled and patted her hand. "You have had quite a time of it," he said, "so I shouldn't wonder if you're a little confused. In the meantime I should be very pleased to have you recover your strength here with me."

"Oh, I couldn't trespass any further on your hospitality!" She tried to lever herself up, but he easily pushed her back down.

"No," he said firmly. "You're far too weak to be up and about. You were half frozen as it was when I found you."

"But I must—"

"Must what? Must arrive for some appointment? How? Do you even know where you were going? Or who would know you there?"

She lowered her head. He was right. She had no idea of anything.

"Besides, you've nothing to wear. Your dress was torn to ribbons."

Heat flooded her face as she realized she must be naked beneath the bedclothes, that he must have seen—everything. He seemed amused by her embarrassment and she bit her lip, suddenly feeling foolish. He was a medical man, after all. And he had saved her life. Would she rather be lying fully clothed and dead in the snow? A tear slipped down her cheek as she murmured a confused mixture of apology and thanks.

He waved his hand, dismissing her words. "My dear girl, there's no sense in distressing yourself further. You just stay here and rest for now, and I'll bring you something to eat later."

"I'm not very hungry."

"You will be."

With that he tucked her arms back beneath the covers and took the candle away. Shadows leapt and danced along the walls as he made his way to the door and closed it gently behind him. She thought she heard the sound of a key turning in the latch but before the idea—and its implications—could take root, she was asleep again.

The fire had died down when next she woke. The sheets were soaked with sweat and she was burning with fever. She kicked away the blankets and lay wholly exposed on the bed: naked, brazen. Her host had drawn the curtains and a jagged stripe of pale light spilled through the trees and lay across the floor. She watched it make its slow way across the room as the moon rose in the sky.

Hunger gnawed at her stomach and her mouth watered. He'd told her she would be hungry. He'd said he would bring her something to eat. Where was he? Should she call out? Knock something else to the floor?

She couldn't lie still. Her skin burned, ached, itched. And there was another kind of hunger, a deeper kind, a kind she'd never known before. She thought of his eyes, his kind smile, his gentle hands. Her skin tingled, weirdly alive and charged like the air before a storm. The blankets beneath her were a sensual pleasure too excruciating to bear and she found herself writhing wantonly, both to escape their caress and to intensify it.

She remembered the wolfsong—the heartrending music of unnatural hunger and need. It had filled her with yearning even as she lay bleeding in the snow. Now she heard it in her mind and she found herself wishing she could join in.

The moonlight had reached the bed, where it spilled over her splayed thighs like quicksilver. Her eyes pierced the darkness. Every detail of the room was discernible to her. She could see each tiny imperfection in the carved oak dressing table, hear the brittle leaves shivering in the trees outside. Most acute of all was her sense of smell. She could smell the rosewater in the washing bowl, the melted wax of the candles in a room farther down the corridor. And she could smell *him*—the hot musky scent of his flesh and his spicy blood beneath.

Her own blood roared in her ears, echoing the surf from somewhere far away. Now she could see the moon fully through the trees—a beacon that drew strange growls from her throat the more she gazed at it. Her fingers clutched at the air, the nail beds burning and making her cry out in a voice that wasn't her own, wasn't even properly a voice.

"Is the pain unbearable?"

She was startled to see him beside her and she wondered how long he'd been there, watching. Time had no meaning. There was only the moonlight and the all-consuming hunger.

She tried to speak, but it was as though her mouth had forgotten how to form words. She shook her head instead and strained toward him, angling her legs as far apart as she could to show him what was *truly* unbearable.

"I brought you something to eat," he said simply. "But first, you will forgive me but I must take some precautions."

He removed his coat and purposefully rolled up his sleeves. Then one by one he unfastened the braided cords that held back the curtains on the bed. He gripped her left wrist firmly and looped the cord around it, knotting it and securing it to the bedpost. Hot desire surged within her and she yanked at the knot, testing its strength. She moaned with pleasure as he bound each limb until she was splayed open on the bed. All the shame and fear she'd felt earlier were gone, and in its place was only hunger.

Once she was immobilized he held up a slice of raw red meat for her to see. Blood dripped from the edges where it had been recently cut. Her heart pounded violently and she lunged for it, held fast by the cords.

With an indulgent smile he held the meat out to her in the palm of his hand, where she tore it to pieces with her teeth, devouring it. Warm blood ran over her chin and down her throat and she was drunk on the pleasure. Nothing had ever tasted so delicious, so satisfying. He placed a hand on the side of her face and she pressed against it, biting gently at the meaty aspect of his palm, running her sharp teeth softly over his skin and licking away the juices.

The moon spilled its icy blue glow into the room. It crawled over and inside her skin, filling her with desire so intense it made her light-headed. She wanted more. She also knew instinctively that more would never be enough.

He stepped back and regarded her. "I don't anticipate a full transformation tonight. It's too soon since..." He paused, then asked, "Can you understand me?"

His words made sense in a distant, abstract way, but she only heard his voice. She wanted to lose herself in its dulcet tones. What she understood more easily was his mood. Beneath his professional demeanor was a hunger of his own. A hunger he was denying.

She strained against her bonds and whimpered, trying to convey her understanding. The ropes bit deeply into her ankles as she raised her hips, offering herself to him. She growled deep in her throat, a ferocious little sound of pure desperation. Beads of sweat stood out across her chest like jewels and her nails clawed at the headboard, carving deep furrows into the wood. She wanted him. And she knew that he wanted her just as much.

But his will was stronger than hers. He pulled a blanket over her, smiling even as he covered her nudity. "You'll sleep now," he said.

She shook her head but the motion made her dizzy. The room grew blurry and she realized that he must have put something in the meat. She fought to stay awake but it was no use; the last thing she registered before sinking into a dreamless sleep was the hope that he would still be there when she woke up.

Birds were shrieking outside and from somewhere close by came a loud rhythmic ticking. She opened her eyes to see that he hadn't left her. He was looking at his pocket watch, and when he noticed that she was awake he snapped it shut. She winced at the sound it made. Everything was so loud, every sense painfully acute.

"It's morning," he said. "You're over the worst of it."

"Worst of what?" she mumbled.

With infinite care he untied her right wrist and held the arm up for her to see. She had recovered her senses enough to be shocked.

Her fingernails had split and lengthened into thick, heavy claws and where before she had seen a patchwork of angry red wounds and stitches across her forearm, there were now only pale pink scars, as though from injuries that had healed years before.

"Your carriage didn't just overturn," he explained. "You were attacked."

She looked up at him fearfully. "Attacked?"

He went to the window and drew the curtains fully open. The sky was strewn with wild color and light, but she had no idea whether it was morning or evening. "Strange creatures live in the forest," he said, his tone a mix of fascination and disquiet. "Creatures I have been studying for many years. When a person is bitten, they become something that belongs neither to this world nor to theirs." He turned to face her. "You have perhaps heard such stories?"

Her eyes widened. "Werewolves," she said at last.

She *had* heard such things as a child but never supposed them to be true. Indeed, if he had said the word to her the night before she'd have thought him mad. Now, however, she could hardly deny what she had experienced. The proof was carved into the headboard like an ancient, arcane map. Memories came to her like fragments of a nightmare: A huge hairy beast leaping from the shadows. The horses rearing, panicking. The carriage tumbling onto its side, spilling her out. A flurry of teeth and claws. Blood and snow. Death. And rebirth.

She knew it to be true. Knew it with an uncanny, animal perception.

He was watching her intently, as though reading her thoughts. "You can never go back," he said, "even if you could remember who you are or where you were going."

Hot tears stung her eyes and she tugged feebly at her bonds. "So I'm a prisoner."

He frowned as though she'd said something vulgar. "Of course not. If you like, you can choose to live among those in the forest, eating squirrels and rabbits, shivering in the winter, hunted by the villagers who believe the forest to be cursed. However, if you would prefer a more comfortable and civilized existence, you are welcome to stay here, where I can look after you."

"As another creature to study, you mean?"

His frown deepened and he looked hurt. "You really won't be helped, will you?"

She sighed and lowered her head, ashamed. "I'm sorry. I shouldn't be so ungrateful."

She stared at her hand, flexing the fingers and marveling at the fearsome claws. They looked as though they were slowly retracting, but they still looked capable of doing damage. The night before, she'd ripped apart the meat he'd given her, not with teeth but with fangs. She ran her tongue along the edge of her teeth and noticed that they, too, had lost some of their animal sharpness. "Am I dangerous?" she wondered aloud.

"Not as you are now," he said and he began to untie the other knots, freeing her limbs. "Right now you're somewhere in between, but still mostly human. However, when the wolf in you takes over she won't know me. She'll have to learn to trust me as any wild animal would."

Her wrists and ankles burned where the cords had bitten into the skin but the red marks faded before her eyes. She gathered the blanket around her and rose from the bed. The fine silk rug on the floor made her bare feet tingle with heightened pleasure. She crossed to the dressing table and met the eyes of the girl in the mirror. Her long dark hair was in disarray, giving her a feral look that seemed at odds with the unnatural grace of her movements.

The wolf had no concept of time or of consequences; it was a creature of pure instinct. It existed entirely in the present. There was no sense in mourning a past she couldn't remember or fearing a future she couldn't know. The wolf wanted only to live in the moment and the moment was undeniably pleasant. Her rescuer really was extraordinarily handsome. Even now, overwhelmed and exhausted by all that had happened, she could feel the primal hunger within, could feel her body stirring again.

"What if someone comes to look for me?" she asked.

He sat on the edge of the bed, watching her. "The villagers

will explain about the tragic accident in the forest. You'll be presumed dead."

"And if they come here? To this house?"

"I'm well respected in the village," he said. "They regard me as an eccentric, but certainly no one would suspect me of anything untoward."

"You live alone?"

"Alone these twenty-five years."

"Then," she said, a teasing smile playing on her lips, "who shall I be when they ask? A girl you found in the woods?" She let the blanket fall from her shoulders. It pooled around her ankles and she stood naked and unashamed before him. From across the room she could hear his heartbeat quicken.

"Shall I be your cherished pet, curled up on the hearth, eating from your hand?" As she spoke she sank to the floor and crept toward him on all fours. She knelt at his feet and rested her chin on his knee as she peered up at him. She placed one hand gently in his lap, pressing her palm against the hardness she found there. "Or shall I be your experimental subject, strapped down in your laboratory, naked and helpless..."

His resolve crumbled. He lifted her by her arms onto the bed, holding her down and crushing his mouth to hers. She arched herself into him, her tongue finding his. Then he pulled away and she gave a little cry of dismay. But it was only so he could remove his clothes, which he did quickly, leaving everything in a heap on the floor. In seconds he was back with her, his warm flesh pressed to hers, his hardness demanding entry.

He took her roughly, hungrily, and she threw back her head with a gasp as he filled her completely, thrusting in and out, every movement an attack—a desperately welcome one. She cried out, hardly recognizing the voice as her own.

She wrapped her legs around him and squeezed them tightly

together, flexing her inner muscles and enjoying his gasp of delight. Her own pleasure was almost overwhelming. She was balanced on a knife-edge of sensations almost too intense to process. Almost. If she were still wholly human she would never be able to endure it. She wanted everything he could give her, everything he could do to her. Pleasure and pain and everything in between.

When the climax overtook them both, she forgot herself completely. His moans mingled with her own wild cries and from deep within her came the urge to sink her sharp teeth into his throat, to make him like her, like them. She could hear the wolves in the woods, howling, as though communing with her from miles away.

Before he could react she writhed out of his grasp and leapt on top of him, pushing him down and raking her claws down his chest. He hissed with pain and met her frenzied eyes with surprise but not fear. She dragged her long pink tongue up the length of him, drunk on the taste of his blood.

But as she bared her teeth to bite he seized her by the arms and forced her down on her front, holding her wrists together in the small of her back with one hand. He yanked the cord from the nearest bedpost and wound it tightly around her wrists, ignoring her yelps of protest.

"Foolish girl!"

She peered up at him from under a curtain of hair, the madness fading with the diminishing pulses of her orgasm.

Panting and spent, he was nonetheless in control of her again. He put his trousers on but frowned at his bleeding chest as he dabbed at it with his shirt. Then he met her eyes and assumed an authoritative tone. "The condition is communicated through a bite and fortunately you've only inflicted a few scratches. It's a nuisance, but I don't think you've done any real damage.

However, if you insist on trying to bite, little wolf, I shall have no choice but to keep you in a cage."

She squirmed at his rebuke, a slave to desire at his every word, however harsh.

He saw her response and his features softened. He stroked her hair with gruff affection. "I'll be in my laboratory. When you've freed yourself you may come and find me." And he left her wrestling with the knots.

He'd tied the cord viciously tight in his annoyance and it took her some considerable time to loosen it. Time enough for him to tend his wounds and forgive her, she hoped. At last the cord went slack and she wriggled free. She sprang lithely to her feet, stretching her limbs and relishing the strange new fluidity of her movements. The immediacy of the wolf's madness had left her, but her memories were strikingly vivid. A deep engulfing soreness burned through every part of her, but it was a welcome pain; it told her she was alive. More alive than she had ever felt before.

She knew exactly where he was because she could smell him. She walked naked up a curving staircase that led her to the top of the house. A forbidding oak door opened onto a laboratory filled with strange contraptions and an array of scientific equipment, things whose purpose she couldn't begin to guess. He stood at a table crowded with bottles of colored liquid and shining steel instruments. He was wringing out a blood-soaked cloth in a bowl of water and she saw that he'd stitched up the worst of the scratches.

She remembered the salty taste of his blood, the velvety thickness of it on her tongue. She traced one ragged wound with a finger, biting her lip guiltily. "Did I really do that?"

He removed her hand and kissed her palm. "You certainly did."

She blushed and looked down at the floor. "I don't know how to apologize," she said, searching for words. "In the moment, I…I just wanted you to be—well, like me."

"I know. But you will have to learn to control yourself, my girl. I meant what I said about the cage." He nodded toward the wall.

A heavy iron cage stood there, large enough for a wolf to pace back and forth in. The thought of being locked inside it sent a little pulse through her sex and she pressed her thighs together. She could see herself growling hungrily at her captor from within, pawing at the massive padlock that hung from the latch. As she touched the smooth cold iron she imagined him stroking her sleek fur through the bars, taming her day by day until he could trust her enough to let her out. She turned back to him as she leaned against the cage, feeling drunk at the thought of his absolute mastery of her. He had saved her from one life and given her a new one—one in which she could not survive without his care.

She braced her palms against the top of the cage and raised herself enough to sit down, gasping a little at the chill of iron against her bare skin. He parted her legs and moved closer, standing between her thighs.

"I don't even have a name," she mused.

"Actually, you do. I've given you one."

She closed her eyes against the nervous flutter of her heart, waiting for him to tell her what it was. Instead he reached across to the cluttered table and held up an elegantly tooled strip of rich brown leather. He looped it around her neck and fastened it with a tiny lock. "You belong to me now," he said, "my pet." Then he pressed the palm of his hand against her warm wet sex.

She whimpered softly as he pushed her back, forcing her

body to arch. Her right foot found purchase on the edge of a cabinet and she held herself still as he kissed her breasts, teasing her nipples into hard little buds with his tongue. She pressed against him, letting him know she wanted more. Much, much more.

He spread her legs apart and drew his fingers down to her sex, slipping two inside her with ease. Then three. With his hand he reached every deep part of her, stroking her and pushing hard against the walls of her sex while she clung to the bars of the cage, surrendering completely. His thumb remained outside, teasing her most sensitive place with a clinician's dexterity. The flood of sensations gathered and swelled until it broke over her in a wave and she gave herself to it with breathless abandon.

When she finally came back to herself he was smiling at her. He gently withdrew his hand. "Extraordinary," he said, sounding both surprised and pleased. "I don't imagine many women would have enjoyed that. I'm sure it warrants further study."

She blushed and lowered her head. "Let me be sure I understand. I heal quickly but you don't. Is that right?"

"Yes."

"So any damage I might sustain, however serious, could be fine again in a couple of days?"

He took her wrist and lifted her arm for her to see. There was now no trace at all of her own injuries. "That has been my observation with previous subjects," he said, emphasizing the word. *Subject.*

Her face burned as she spoke, giving voice to unearthly desires. "Then it really doesn't matter how rough you are with me."

"No. It doesn't."

"Then perhaps you could show me"—she teased the drawer open with her toes and her eyes gleamed with reflected light from the stainless steel instruments nestled inside—"what you use these for."

His fingers dance over the keys, filling the room with music as he works his way through the sonata. The final notes linger and then fade into silence as he looks down at the wolf that lies at his feet. She raises her head to meet his gaze and licks his proffered hand. He runs his finger along the line of her spine and the little silver lock jingles at her throat as she rises to his touch. Moonlight streams in through the windows and her amber eyes shine with anticipation. He releases the chain that tethers her to the leg of the piano. The collar and chain are no longer a necessity, but he enjoys the deep submission they bring out in her.

She pads softly at her master's feet as he leads her outside to greet the moon. She likes to make the change outside, in the snow. The snow reminds her of the first time. When the snow is gone she will change among the flowers. Then the falling leaves.

He unfastens the chain from her collar and she bounds down the stone steps into the frozen garden. The moon reveals itself through a veil of clouds and he stands watching the wolf as she capers in the snow. Soon the wild circles of paw prints will be intertwined with human footprints and he will go to her then. She will be frightened at first, bewildered to find herself suddenly standing naked in the snow. Then she will remember. And he will take her back inside to spend the night reminding her of everything else.

COVER HIM
WITH DARKNESS

Janine Ashbless

The first time I saw him fettered there in the dark, I wept.

I was seven years old. My father led me by the hand down the steps behind the church altar, through a passage hewn into the mountainside. I'd never been permitted through that door before. Inside, there were niches cut into the rock walls, and near the church they were filled with painted and gilded icons of the saints and of Our Lord, but farther back those gave way to statuettes of blank-eyed pagan gods, growing cruder in execution and less human in appearance as we walked on. I clung to Father's hand and cringed from the darkness. Finally we came out into a roofless chamber, where the walls leaned inward a hundred feet over our heads and the floor was nothing but a mass of loosely tumbled boulders. I looked up, blinking at the light that seemed blinding, though in fact this was a dim and shadowed place. I could see a wisp of cloud against the seam of blue and the black speck of a mountain eagle soaring across the gap.

There he lay upon a great tilted slab of limestone, his wrists and ankles bound by twisted leather ropes whose farther ends seemed to be set into the rock itself. It was hard to say whether the slab had always been underground or had fallen long ago from the mountain above; our country is, after all, much prone to earthquakes. Dirt washed down with the rain had stained him gray, but I could make out the muscled lines of his bare arms and legs and the bars of his ribs. There was an old altar cloth draped across his lower torso; only much later did I realize that Father had done that, to spare his small daughter the man's nakedness.

"Here, Milja," said my father, pushing me forward. "It is time you knew. This is the charge of our family. This is what we guard day and night. It is our holy duty never to let him be found or escape."

I was only little: he looked huge to me; huge and filthy and all but naked. I stared at the thongs, as thick as my skinny wrist, knotted cruelly tight about his broader ones. They stretched his arms above his head so that one hand could not touch the other, and they held his ankles apart. I felt a terrible ache gather in my chest. I pressed backward, into Father's black robes.

"Who is he?" I whispered.

"He is a very bad man."

That was when the prisoner moved for the first time. He rolled his head and turned his face toward us. I saw the whites of his eyes gleam in his gray face. Even at seven, I could read the suffering and the despair burning there. I squirmed in Father's grip.

"I think he is hurt," I whimpered. "The ropes are hurting him."

"Milja," said Father, dropping to his knees and putting his arm around me. "Don't be fooled—this is not a human being. It just looks like one. Our family has guarded him here since the first people came to these mountains. Before the Communists. Before the Turks. Before the Romans, even. He has always been here. He is a prisoner of God."

"What did he do?"

"I don't know, little chick."

That was when I began to cry.

"What did he do?" became a question I repeated many times as I grew up, along with "Who is he?" My father did not lie, but nor could he answer my question truthfully. He was an educated man, though he was now the priest of an isolated village in the most barren, mountainous corner of our rugged country. He had studied engineering at university in Belgrade, but he admitted that the answers to my queries were unclear to him. "The gods have condemned him," he would say, with a sigh. That sounded so strange coming from an Orthodox priest that I didn't know what to think.

Every Sunday, after going down into the village to celebrate the Divine Liturgy there—nobody ever climbed up the two hundred steps to our dingy little church carved into the sheer rock—he would descend into the prison. He would take the man water and bread, and wash his face. My father was not without compassion, even for a prisoner, and he felt the dignity of his position.

"Is he...Prometheus?" I asked when I was ten and had been reading the Greek myths in one of the dog-eared encyclopedias Father had brought from the capital. "The gods chained up Prometheus forever. Is it him?"

"It may be."

"But...Prometheus was *good*, Father. He taught us how to be civilized. He stole fire from the gods to bring it to men. He was on our side!"

"What did man do with fire, Milja?"

"Cook?"

"He smelted iron, little chick, and with iron he made swords. He made all the weapons of war, and men have slaughtered men in countless millions ever since. Are you sure Prometheus had our best interests at heart? Would we not have been happier if we had stayed in the Stone Age?"

I was too young to answer that. Father sighed and fetched a black-bound book, laying it on the table by the window where the light could fall upon it. He opened it to near the beginning.

"My grandfather told me that it is Azazel we hold in our keeping. Have you heard of him?"

"No," said I in a small voice.

"No man or titan, but a demon, little chick. A leader of the fallen angels: those Sons of God who lusted after mortal women. The Israelites dedicated their scapegoat sin-offering to him. Like the Greeks' Prometheus, he too is credited with teaching men metalworking and warcraft—and women the arts of seduction and sorcery. Here in the Book of Enoch, see; the angel Raphael is commanded: 'bind Azazel hand and foot and cast him into the darkness. And lay upon him rough and jagged rocks, and cover him with darkness, that he may remain there forever.'"

"Which is right, then?" I asked. "Is he a demon or is he Prometheus?"

"Maybe he is both, and it's the same story. Or maybe he is something else altogether. All I know is that he's been here since the beginning, and that it is our duty to keep him bound. It's what our forefathers dedicated their lives to. And you must carry on when I am gone, Milja. You must marry and teach your husband and your sons, so that it is never forgotten. And you must *never* tell anyone else, all your life. It must not go beyond the family. Promise me!"

"Why not?

"What if someone, someone who did not understand, felt sorry for him and set him free? What if he is one of the great demons, Milja? What would happen to this world?"

I was eleven when I started to visit him in secret. I took him food, because I couldn't bear any longer to lie awake in bed thinking of how hungry he must be. I knew he could get water—when it rained it would run down the rocks onto his face—but at eleven I was always ravenous myself, and it seemed the worst of tortures. And the image of him lying bound there haunted my dreams more and more, evoking feelings I had no words for—not then—until it seemed impossible for me to stay away.

Still, I went at midday, when the light was strongest. I brought him bread crusts and cheese. I picked berries from the mountain bushes and fed them between his cracked lips.

I remember the first time I did it; the first time I went alone. I climbed up on that big rock slab and knelt over his dirt-streaked body, and he opened his eyes and looked up into mine. His irises were so dark that in this half-light they looked like holes.

"What's your name?" I whispered.

I don't know if he heard me. He certainly didn't reply. He just looked at me, from the depths of his private torment.

"I brought you some milk." I tipped the teat of the little skin of goat's milk to his lips and let it trickle into the side of his mouth, carefully: I was scared of choking him. His throat worked and his lips twitched, bleeding. He drank it all and I sat back. That was when, with obvious and painful effort, the lines of his face pulled into a brief smile—a smile so fragile a butterfly might have trampled it underfoot.

That was when I was lost.

* * *

I was fourteen when I first heard him speak.

"Milja," he murmured, greeting me. His voice was hoarse from disuse. I nearly fled.

"What's your name?" I asked again, but he didn't answer. He only twisted from one hip to the other to ease the strain on his back and hissed with pain. The power of his corded body, terrible even under constraint, made me tremble.

He spoke only rarely in the years that followed, and what he said made little sense to me—often not even in any language I knew, and when I could make out the words they seemed to be nothing but fragments. "Leaves on the brown-bright water..." he might mutter to himself. I think he was remembering things he had seen before he was imprisoned. As I grew to realize how the uncountable years had stolen even his mind, I felt dizzy with horror.

I was eighteen when Father sent me away.

You have to understand; I grew up alone, set apart from the other village children. Oh, when I was a little child I ran and played with them, but as I grew older things changed. Our family had been here for centuries before the village was founded, fulfilling our ancient duty, until war and turmoil and expanding horizons had scattered and dwindled its numbers. We had always been treated as separate from the rest of the village; sometimes we would intermarry, but only our boys choosing their girls. I was the last of the line to grow up here. Schooling in the village was little more than rudimentary, and at twelve I was the only girl still being taught: all the others my age were laboring with their mothers in the house and the fields. At sixteen I was still studying under my father's tutelage and had become a freak in the eyes of the whole community. The girls turned as one and cut me off from their company, erecting a wall of sneering hostility. The boys just teased me unremittingly, their curiosity expressed in the crudest manner—thrown stones were the least of my worries.

I think Father was secretly pleased I showed no interest in the village boys. He hoped I would go to university some day, like him.

Perhaps I should have understood them more and tried to make friends. Perhaps. But I was young, and I thought all men should be like my gentle, scholarly father, so I was alone a great deal. I looked after the house when Father was out; his ability to fix generators and rotavators was something the townspeople valued him for as much as his priestly status, I think. I cooked and did the laundry. I read. I climbed the hillsides on my own, being careful to avoid the shepherds up there. And I went to visit our prisoner, every day.

As I grew older I grew bolder too. I stole wine for him. I baked him honey cake. I would bring water to wash the grime off his body, slightly shocked by my own recklessness as I wiped down the heavy slabs of his muscles, or lifted a lower leg so that I might massage his calf and relieve the ache of his trapped limbs to some tiny extent. Sometimes he would focus upon my face long enough to whisper my name.

His body fascinated me. I learned its illicit contours in the half-dark, mostly by touch. He felt cold all over, like the rock he lay on, but there were smooth bits and there were places rough with hair. There were harder and softer stretches. There was a big, jagged scar over the right side of his abdomen, but it looked old. There were things only a married woman should see.

I wanted to take his pain away.

I was book-smart, as they say in America—there was no such phrase in our village, though they understood the concept perfectly—and I was burning with curiosity, and not wise. One day I lay down beside him on the stone and nested my head on his chest. I could hear the slow beat of his heart. With my right hand I drew off the cloth that preserved his modesty, and for the first time I touched him without the excuse that I was washing him. Without any excuse at all.

I took his male member in my hand. Tentatively I began to caress it.

He responded to that. Not just the flesh in my grasp, but his whole body—his back arching, his breath catching in his throat, his toes flexing and curling. I was terrified and thrilled. He groaned deep in his chest and I felt it through my bones. His breath started to come harder and faster, with a little tremble at the end of each exhalation, interspersed with murmured, unintelligible words.

I stroked him until he was hard and not cold at all. Until he was so eager that he was too thick for my grasp. My unpracticed hand began to ache with the effort and I stopped for rest.

"Milja!" he groaned, desperate.

Impelled by a strange and burning instinct, I sat up then and lifted my skirt so that I could straddle him. His hair tickled up against my bare thighs. Now I could study him stretched out beneath me, his muscles straining against their tethers and his member stuck out in front of me, angled over his stomach. Now I could get both hands on it; now I could stroke him properly, from root to crown.

So heavy. So strong. My hands embraced that hardness. He came all across his belly, spurting between my fingers, crying out in his strange language. He was beautiful in a way I couldn't understand and had never anticipated: so beautiful I felt it as pain. I stroked him gently as he subsided, my own body a cauldron of conflicting needs and fears.

I was careful to clean him up afterward, but my attempts to cover my tracks made no difference. My father was waiting in the church when I climbed the passageway to the light once more, his arms folded across his chest.

"Milja! What have you been doing?"

I couldn't answer. My skin burned with shame, proclaiming my guilt. I felt like there was no air in my lungs.

Father's brows were knotted in anger, as if he were the Patriarch Moses surveying the sinning Israelites when he came down the mountain. "Didn't I tell you, child, that Azazel is the teacher of seduction? Did you not hear what I said?"

I bit my lip and wondered if I was going to be sick.

"I will send you away, Milja. You cannot stay near him. Your cousin Vera is in Boston, America: I will send you to her."

I was twenty-five when I saw him again.

I went to Boston, as my father arranged. He sold several of the icons and statues from within the cave to pay for me; there's never any shortage of black-market buyers for that sort of thing. Wheels were greased. I went to college. I graduated as a structural engineer and got a good job.

I was even engaged to be married, for a while. Father was delighted.

Ben was a young man I met at college, and he was in a student metal band called Loki Unbound. The name of the group was the only reason I went to watch their gig: it turned out that the Scandinavians have their own story of a wicked god who defied the other gods and was imprisoned in torment beneath the earth forever, bound there with the sinews of his own son. Their version says that when he escapes, it will be the end of the world.

Despite his metal aspirations, Ben was really quite sweet.

And I was a good girl from the old country, so we didn't sleep together until we were engaged. It didn't work out well: on our third night I begged to tie him up, spread-eagled on the bed. Then I straddled him, slipping his cock into my hungry embrace. Below me, in the warm, dim light of the candles we'd lit, his body lay stretched out like a sacrifice: narrow hips, long fawn hair, elbows raised as he braced against the scarves knotted at his wrists.

A stray thought grazed my mind: a wish that he had darker hair, and more of it on his torso. But it was only momentary, a twist in the rising surge of my appetite. I clenched my inner muscles to make him gasp, and then I used my thighs to slide up and down on his cock, angling it deep inside me. Every time my clit ground against him a wave of heat seemed to billow up from the point where we were joined, filling me to the bursting point. My vision grew blurred. I tugged at my nipples, grinding them between my fingers. Ben bucked beneath me, thrusting upward to impale my sex, trying to fill the need he saw in me—but without the slightest idea of how great and hollow and ancient was that void in my soul.

For a moment, I didn't see Ben or the bed. I saw a great slab of rock, and a man without a name, and my wails seemed to echo back from stone walls as I slammed down upon him, burning with the ferocity of my orgasm, my face distorted with pain.

"Whoa," he said. "Jesus, Milja."

I burst into tears and struck at him, howling.

Ben freaked out then. We never got as far as a fourth time.

But I tried my best not to think about the prisoner, as I studied and made friends and buried myself in my work. What would be the point, when Father would not let me go home—not until I was safely married? And to be honest it was easy to forget, because in Boston it all seemed entirely unreal: not just the cavern and the bound man isolated in darkness, but the silent little church and the mountain village. It seemed like a story, something from a movie I'd watched as a child. America was loud and roaring with life, and its steel and glass and crowds and wide horizons filled me to the brim, leaving no room for memories. I loved my new world.

But I dreamt about him. I dreamt about him stretched out, shifting hopelessly the few inches permitted by his bonds, in a desperate attempt to relieve his aching muscles. I dreamt he stared into the darkness and stretched back his head and called my name, and that he told me everything about himself: secrets always forgotten when I woke. I dreamt about him shivering under the snow of our brutal winters, and choking in the flash floods of spring. And every morning for seven years I woke with my pillow wet with the tears I'd cried in my sleep.

Then one day Vera told me that Father was ill, and that I had been called home. Back I flew across the ocean, Vera at my side—she was old enough to be my mother, and I had no one else to take that role. We were driven up into the mountains in the back of a truck, bouncing along rutted roads beneath beetling cliffs. The village had changed very little, I thought, though there were more abandoned houses, and the ones that were still occupied sported huge ugly satellite dishes on their tiled roofs. I had changed far more. I could see it reflected in the stares of others as I climbed down from the vehicle: me with my tight jeans and my makeup, with my sunglasses and my looped plastic necklace. The old women in their black dresses and their headscarves, fluttering around Father's borrowed sickbed, tutted at me and muttered to each other as if I couldn't understand the things they said.

Father wasn't even in his own bed: he had collapsed in the village and it had been impossible to take him up the long climb to our isolated house. He too had changed: his big black beard was gray now, his face thin and bony. I was shocked: he was only sixty but in this country he was an old man.

I don't want to remember those days. I felt as though every fiber in my body was screaming.

We wanted to take Father to a hospital in the capital straightaway, but he wouldn't hear of it. Vera appointed herself head nurse, infuriating all the old women, and slowly his strength rallied. He agreed to go for medical treatment—but only if I stayed. "Someone," he whispered to me, plucking at the sheet over his chest, "someone from the family must stay and guard him. It is our holy duty." He gripped my hand. "If you have to leave…I have wired the cave with explosive. The switch is in the passage. You must bring the walls down on him."

My throat closed up so I could hardly breathe.

It was not until my father was safely in a taxi with Vera that I made the climb up to our old house. Every step was familiar, and yet everything was strange. I was seeing now with the eyes of a foreigner: the tumbledown buildings wedged under the brow of the cliff; the soot-blackened interior of the tiny church with its icons so darkened by age that only their gilt halos could be made out; the narrow, padlocked door behind the altar. I retrieved the key from under its floor tile and stepped into the passage beyond for the first time in years. I couldn't have grown much taller since eighteen, but the roof felt lower. The church's lingering scent of frankincense gave way to damp stone: a cellar smell.

Down I went, into the dark, the first person in well over a month to tread this path. I carried only a two-liter bottle of water and a flashlight.

There. There he was. My nightmares were all real. I felt my heart pound against my ribs like it would smash them.

I was seeing him with adult eyes too. He didn't look like a titan, or a demon, or a god. He looked like a man: perhaps in his early thirties, with an athletic build and dark hair going prematurely gray. Tall, but not remarkably so. Dirty; naked; abused. His exposed armpits and crotch were exclamation marks of vulnerability. I picked my way over to the slab and knelt over him. His face was just the same as it had been seven and more years ago: stubbled, haggard with pain but handsome despite that. Breathtakingly so, like the agonized beauty of certain icons.

I touched his face. He opened his eyes. "Milja."

I began to cry.

"You came back."

I was shocked: he'd never addressed me before. The words "I'm sorry!" spilled from my lips along with my sobs; "Oh, god, oh, god—I'm sorry!"

"He said…he had sent you away. I was so afraid…you would not return."

My tears were dripping on his face. I wiped clumsily at them, smearing the dirt. "What's your name?" I begged.

He didn't answer.

"Who are you?"

He tried to moisten his lips. "I…don't remember."

Bending forward, I pressed my wet cheek to his. Did I believe him? I don't know. He could be Loki or Prometheus or Azazel; I know I didn't care anymore. When I sat up I reached to the nape of my neck and undid my necklace. The sheath of bright blue plastic peeled off to reveal a supple length of steel-toothed metal: a wire saw.

I cut through his bonds. It took a long time.

He sat up as I freed his last ankle, tugging the severed ends of his tethers loose and rubbing at his foot. His breath came harsh and shallow: I think the change in posture was agonizing. I passed him the water bottle but I had to open it for him as he had no idea about screw-top caps. The water escaped down his throat and chest as he glugged it back, cutting runnels in the dirt there. I was wearing a long skirt that day to mollify the old women; I wet the hem while he was getting his breath back and tried to gently clean his face with the cloth.

That was rash. He caught my hand with his; I felt the fingers of his other hand on my bare calf. Our eyes locked, and I felt time hang, breathless—before he moved to cover my mouth with his, and I tasted blood and stone and darkness in his kiss.

There were no words. There had never been adequate words for his pain and need, or for my hunger. All these years my guilt and my loneliness had pulled me back to this place and to this moment: this kiss. I clasped his neck and felt the play of his muscles in his shoulders as we moved together; there was grit stuck to the skin of his shoulders that might have been there for centuries, and I brushed it away with my fingertips. I yielded to his lips and his arms and the press of his torso, repudiating my yesterdays and throwing away all my tomorrows in the rush of this moment, this ache, this rapture. He had already taken my heart: now he stole my breath and my senses. When he broke the kiss I cried out in loss.

Then I reached down, tentative and trembling, to stroke the rising stake of his cock. I couldn't stop myself. He was just as big as I remembered.

In response he slithered to the edge of the rock and pulled me down flat upon it as he stooped over me. The stone was cold and hard at my shoulders; in the discomfort I felt a dim echo of his agony and I welcomed it. His hands were clumsy in their eagerness, desperate to be gentle. He pushed my blouse up to my armpits and—clearly having no clue what to do with my bra—

shoved that out of the way in similar fashion so that he could bury his face in my bare breasts. His kisses were ravenous; I could feel him shaking under my hands. My nipples, wet from his mouth, hardened like gemstones in the chill cavern air. He licked me all the way down my stomach as if he was devouring me alive, filling his mouth and nose up with my scent and my warmth, gasping between kisses. Then he bunched my skirt up at my waist and caressed my legs, his hands strong and forceful, yanking the wisp of lace between them aside so that he could drop to his knees and sink his face into my sex. His stubble rasped on my inner thighs. As his tongue settled over my clit I spasmed and arched, twisting away from him and thrusting into him all at the same time, overwhelmed by his mouth. He pinned me, and I yielded joyfully. His fingers spread me as he kissed and sucked and licked. My whimpers of pleasure became frantic, and his attentions grew even more desperate; I was being eaten by a starving man.

Soaring on the storm of my arousal, I wrapped my fingers in his hair, tugging.

"Come here! Please...oh, god, please!"

He lifted his head and I drew him up over me. Now I could see, in the dim light, the thick bar of his erection. Just for a moment, anyway—before he buried it between my raised thighs, entering me.

Oh. This was what I had been dreaming of. Seven years of dreams.

Braced on his arms, wrapped in my legs, he gasped my name over and over as he thrust. I had no name to cry out in answer. I just wailed without words as I began to come, my voice echoing off the rocks, and I heard his guttural barks of effort under my cries as he slammed home, pouring his need into me, filling me to overflowing with semen and release.

Then, afterward, he stooped over me to kiss my face. His lips were warm now, his skin damp and salty. When he rose from me his body gleamed. In the half-light I saw the slow shake of his head and the glint of his bared teeth. He stretched, flexing each joint, and just by watching I felt the inexpressible pleasure of being able to stand and twist and stretch every muscle: the visceral joy of freedom. He laughed disbelievingly, low in his throat.

"Which way out?" he asked, reaching to pull me to my feet. My legs were weak and I tipped against him, dizzy.

"I'll show you."

I led him to the tunnel mouth, but he wasn't content to follow and he pushed ahead, drawing me by the hand. He didn't spare the icons and the votive offerings a single glance: his attention was fixed upon escape. As the first breath of warmer air came to us he released me and hurried forward, fending off the walls as he stumbled because his legs were still a little uncertain beneath him.

I felt then the clutch of fear. He didn't look back to see if I was following. He didn't seem to remember me. All his focus was on what lay before him and, as I hurried to keep up, every straining inch of the distance between us tore at me.

Was he going to abandon me, now that I'd freed him?

The door to the church was standing open. He surged out into the room, searching for an exit. I wondered for a moment whether he would be able to cross holy ground, but he didn't even seem to notice his surroundings: he had eyes for nothing but the outer door, its ancient planks outlined by the sun. He wrenched it open and the blazing glow of the afternoon poured in upon him, lapping his naked flesh, haloing him in light. A human would have flinched and shielded his eyes: even where I stood, at the back of the chamber, I was half-blinded. Tears swelled my eyes and my throat. He only blinked, staring.

The breath stopped in my breast as I waited for what would happen next—for him to burn to ash perhaps, or for an eagle to swoop down upon him from the heavens. Or for him to unfurl demon wings and vanish with a clap of sulfurous thunder. I didn't even have his name to call out in my terror.

None of those things happened. Instead he looked back into the room, toward me, and stretched out his hand. His eyes pleaded. I moved to lay my fingers in his and he pulled me against him, holding me tight. I could feel his strong, hard body trembling. Without words we stood holding each other, looking out upon the valley and the village below, with its fields and its tiled roofs and the snow-capped karst peaks beyond: the terrifying open vistas of freedom.

A ROSE IN THE WILLOW GARDEN

Elizabeth Daniels

Do you think the dead come back and watch the living?"

The bartender's attention slid from the glass he was polishing to the cherry-jeweled glass of ginger ale by Bierce's hand, then back again.

"Dude, I have no idea. But whatever you're taking, don't take any more of it in here."

Bierce mentally shrugged. Typical. Not that he cared. The attempt at conversation was only for show and the question was rhetorical, anyway.

He swirled the liquid in his glass and sipped, absently pretending to peruse the gumdrop-colored liquors lined up in front of the antique bar mirror. The patrons here liked their drinks as bright as their clothing was dark. When the bartender had turned away, Bierce shifted his posture until he could watch the ebb and flow of the crowd, stutter-stopping on the faces of the women. Most, he skipped over. Only on a few did his gaze linger as he tried to look past the patina of makeup and self-conscious clothing to see *it*: the guttering spark, the muted gleam that told him when he'd found what he sought. The half-uneasy, half-intrigued glances that came his way in return he ignored.

Meticulous as always, he surveyed the room once more. This time, he noticed someone staring at him, a young woman with dyed black hair and luscious magnolia curves overflowing a tight black bustier. Seeing she had his attention, she dipped her finger in her wine, brought the glistening digit to her mouth and, inch by inch, sucked its length between her deep red lips.

She was lovely even if she was crude, he had to admit, bursting with youth and health, vibrant with sex. Unfortunately for her, she was also common. He saw women like her every time he hunted, women who wanted him for the night but would not court death to remain with him. He pitied her, knowing his rejection meant she would have to go the way of all other flesh, but he couldn't save everyone.

Not that he'd been able to save anyone, of late. His gloom deepened. Six months of fruitless searching. Maybe it was time to move again.

Sliding from his chair, Bierce paid for his drink and picked up the red rose he'd bought from the bar's flower seller. He considered throwing it to the brunette, since he'd found no use for it at the bar, but why give her false hope when she was not worthy? Instead, he took the rose with him and sauntered into the night.

The river cooled the air just enough to make his leather jacket bearable. Bierce shoved his hands into his pockets and followed the riverwalk to a marshy path winding through a dilapidated park. Most of the globe lights were missing in the old-fashioned fixtures. Those that remained formed a broken string of pearls, scattered along the slope of the hill down to the edge of a small pond. The full moon drowned in the pond's dark depths. It was a perfect hunter's night.

Except Bierce was sick of hunting, especially since he'd become so dissatisfied with the results. He knew other hunters in the park didn't feel the same. He could hear some in the bushes. He strode by, indifferent. A lion had nothing to fear from hyenas.

If only he did not have to hunt. But what other choice did he have? Though he'd tried across the country, suitable quarry had become increasingly elusive, while his own capture had become more difficult to evade. The past six months was the longest he'd gone in years without finding anyone suitable.

Eventually, he would be caught. He had no illusions on that score. Society at large would never understand his gifts, but as long as his recipients did, that was all that mattered.

If only those he'd cherished would not grow so distant after they had received his gift. If only one would linger to be his forever, close enough to touch. He'd never hunt again.

Lost in thought, he was almost upon the girl before he saw her. She sat upon the knee of a huge old weeping willow, swinging her feet like a carefree child and flexing her bare toes in the water. As he approached, she looked up and smiled.

Bierce stopped. Stared. He wasn't certain he had the breath to do anything else. It wasn't that she was beautiful; the moonlight was bright, but not so bright that he could see many details. But he could feel her. What he felt was—hope. He'd never been around anyone who glowed like that, so radiant, so unashamed. Ennui, boredom; studiedly hip, dismissive—these he knew. Hope wasn't fashionable, wasn't modern. On her, it was dazzling.

He stepped closer to her, keeping his pose nonthreatening, but staying close enough to send a message to the other hunters abroad in the night. The lion was gauging his prey, and if the hyenas knew what was good for them, they would go scavenge elsewhere. He heard stealthy rustling as one did just that, and the night grew still.

"Beautiful night." He didn't move, didn't dare let his eagerness slip from the leash.

"Yes, it is." She tilted her head back, letting the moonlight bathe her throat, then straightened. "I always come out for the full moon. It's my time."

"I know what you mean."

She swung her legs again. Her outfit was of a type popular among both the goth and steampunk crowds, a white sleeveless camisole and full petticoat. She must have come from the bar he'd just left. How could he have missed her?

Ruffles foamed around her slim calves as she kicked at the water. "Come sit with me."

"Are you sure you want that?" Bierce tried on a disarming smile; found to his surprise that it was genuine. "You don't even know me."

"*Dites-moi qui vous aimez, et je vous dirai qui vous êtes,*" she said. "Isn't that pretty? It's French. It means 'tell me whom you love, and I'll tell you who you are.' I read it on a tombstone, once."

"I don't like tombstones. They're like bookends to spent lives, trapping the person inside."

"I wouldn't know if they trap people or not. I never had one." Though she still smiled, her eyes were fixed on his face. Hungry. Hopeful.

A thread of kinship spun between them. Here was someone who wanted what he had to offer. Finally. His thoughts whirled and then dropped neatly into order. His hunt was proving successful, after all. Maybe she was even *the* one.

No. He wouldn't get ahead of himself. He took a deep breath, relaxing into relief. This was familiar territory now, and he knew what to do. Making his way around the marshy ground, he sat down beside her, close enough to feel his body heat reflect back from her, not quite close enough to touch. Not yet.

"For you," he said, handing her the rose. Their fingers brushed as she accepted it. Her expression altered.

"Thank you," she said, a slight catch in her voice.

"Thank you for accepting it."

Still holding his gaze, she raised the flower to her mouth and kissed it. He felt another strand of affinity connect and wax between them. Unlike all the others, she, he felt, understood it symbolized his gift and wasn't just a gift itself.

"Bierce Caldwell," he said, extending a hand.

"Rose. Rose Connolly." The hand that took his felt solid but fragile, like a dried flower. Instead of shaking his hand, she wove her fingers between his and held it. Her skin was cold. Not surprising, given her attire, which, he now noticed, was damp. The thin batiste showcased the generous cleft between her breasts and tented neatly over the thrust of her nipples, but veiled their color.

"Did you take a swim?"

She busied herself with his hand, caressing the palm with her flower in a way that made him begin to rise and harden in anticipation. "I was in the water, earlier."

"Would you like my jacket?"

"No." She drew his hand to her chest and slid it beneath the edge of her camisole, curving palm and fingers around the soft, yielding breast beneath its folds. Her flesh warmed as it molded to his. The eyes she turned to his reflected not the silvered moonlight, but the drowning pool beneath. The rose fell, forgotten, to the water. "I want you."

* * *

Making love to Rose on the grassy bank beneath the willow was a kind of decadence Bierce had never experienced. Not the modern connotation of the word, hinting at decay, but old-fashioned, delicious sin. Like the difference between a richly red but rotting strawberry and one that was gushing ripe, bursting flavor on the tongue. Like Rose herself.

He hadn't intended to take her there, not in public, even if it was the middle of the night. He never permitted himself to get carried away, never did anything that might cause him to be captured. He owned the control in his courtships. From the moment he touched Rose, he could no longer plan or calculate. The shock of recognition, the feeling of a kindred spirit, had to be confirmed with a physical connection. From the moment she pressed into him, he could not wait. Nor, judging by her eagerness, could she.

Petticoats became a layered tent over his head and shoulders. He coaxed her open to him with tongue and fingers. The fabric trapped and concentrated her scent, a mingling of sea-salted sweetness and rosewater.

Pleasuring a woman with his mouth was usually something he did out of duty, though he did have a certain pride in his skill. For Rose, it was different. He cultivated her with tender tongue-tip touches of encouragement until her sex began to open to him. Bit by bit, he discovered her: the lightly thatched verge of outer lips, the crumpled petal softness of the inner ones, her entrance, beginning to brim with readiness, then the little thrust of her clitoris. Only then did he taste her, sliding his tongue deep until she rose up against him, crying his name.

Unable to wait any longer, he pushed back the petticoats and took her, gritting his teeth as her tightness split open around him. Only when she tensed and cried out did he realize what that meant. He'd never been a woman's first lover. When he would have withdrawn, she wouldn't let him. He did what he could to make it better, sucking the cold water from her wet nipples and caressing her until she relaxed. He never spilled inside a woman, but he did, for Rose. It was the one thing, the only thing, she demanded of him.

She turned her face from his kiss but curled into him, her embrace more fierce than tender. He rested his cheek on her breast and watched the moon float to the surface of the water. Sated. Comforted. And a little sad, as he always was at this point in a courtship, because one of the three times he would permit himself to have with her was already gone.

Tears tracked slowly down her cheeks. He kissed them away, tasting salted wine on his tongue.

Don't weep, love, he told her silently. *You're mine now. One day you'll come away with me, deep into the dark, and you'll never leave me again.*

As if she could hear him, he heard her whisper, "Oh, if only you meant that."

He dozed, another thing he never did with a woman, much less in such an exposed place. When he woke, she was gone, and a fine, soft drizzle had begun to fall. With a hunter's patience, he dressed and waited until dawn. When the park began to stir to life around him, he walked home in the thickening fog.

Back in his apartment, he began the daily ritual.

From a carved sandalwood box, he carefully removed a double handful of plastic bags, twenty-three in all, each neatly labeled in his machinelike printing. Each containing a photograph of a woman's face and a lock of hair, tenderly coiled. Each woman bore the same tattoo of blue bruises around the throat, sisters with the same death mark. The mark of his gift.

Come away with me, he'd said to each of them. And they had.

Waiting in the bottom of the box was a black silk scarf. He ran the sinuous length through his fingers with care, remembering how it had graced each lovely neck, then looped it around his own. A well-trained snake, it slithered obediently into place. He tied its tail to a hook on the wall.

Last, the summoning. He knew the process to be even more dangerous than hunting his loves, even found it distasteful, but it was the only way he knew to walk the border between life and death, if only for a short time.

Leaning into the scarf's snug coils, he primed himself with efficient, joyless strokes. His climax welled, then burst through the pinprick of consciousness left open, forced by the pressure into a gushing cataract. The room swam away in darkness.

Only then did they appear to him, their images flickering and mute, like vamps of the silent screen. Sarah, shaking out her froth of blonde hair. Emma, flashing perfect teeth in a smile. The beautiful swan curve of Mary's neck and the graceful flutter of her small hands. The others stood behind those three, a crowd of insubstantial images, growing paler by the second.

You're mine, he reassured the shades. *I've protected you. You'll always be beautiful, never grow old or fall prey to disease or harm. If only you will stay with me, I'll always keep you safe.*

But when he loosened the scarf for a draft of air, as always, they turned as one and vanished.

Reality, when it returned, was a costly apartment, scrupulously clean, echoingly bare of anything but the most basic necessities. The scarf lay in a lank, spent length around his shoulders.

And there was Bierce himself, kneeling like a penitent. He did not find that wrong. Lonely as it was, he was always the savior, not the one saved.

He rented a small Arabian Nights–style tent and set it up by the water's edge. He brought blankets. More roses. Music. At moonrise, he built a fire at the water's edge and waited. As the full moon touched the water, she emerged from behind the big willow tree, once again wearing her camisole and petticoats. Only discipline kept him from growing weak with relief. He had half feared she would not return. She gathered her skirts and ran across the grass to him, laughing.

"Did you do this?" She all but danced around the tent. "It's beautiful!"

"Where have you been?"

The question came out more sharply than he had intended, but she didn't seem to mind.

"I can't come until the moon is high. I would have told you before, but I didn't know you would be here again." She stood on tiptoe to kiss the mottled blue bruises at his throat. He closed his eyes, fighting fear and desire. Invoked discipline. Control.

"Were you at a club? You're dressed for it again."

"A club?" She seemed honestly bewildered. "No."

He relaxed a little more. He wanted to tell her how frightened he had been that she would not come back. How he feared for her outside the sphere of his protection. If he did, he knew he would scare her. Her presence helped. He could feel it healing the ache of being separated from her. The intensity of what he felt surprised him. Usually he did not grow so attached until after a second encounter. Rose was rare indeed.

"You're very much like William," she said. Reaching up, she touched his face and hair. "Not in appearance. He was very fair and you're so dark. But you love like he did, I think."

Her words set jealousy simmering. "Who is William? Your boyfriend?"

"My fiancé. Or he was." He recognized sorrow and bewildered hurt in her tone. "His father told him he had to give me up, because a poor girl like me would ruin him. I think it drove him mad. He could never bear to give anything up, not money, not love."

"So it's over?"

She looked away, her mouth pinching. "Oh, yes. Long ago, now."

Bierce gripped her arm. His fingers seemed to sink into the flesh as if it were half mist. "I'm not William and you're not his. You're mine."

For a second, he feared he had ruined everything. Try as he might, he knew he projected an intensity that could be frightening. Every other woman he had courted would have run away screaming into the night. Some of them had.

Rose looked from the deep dimples of his fingers in her skin up to his face. And smiled.

"Show me."

The words were challenge and permission. Bierce's internal leashes snapped like threads. Dragging her into the tent, he threw her onto the pile of blankets and fell beside her, shoving his knee between her legs. Clothing fell away, torn, his as well as hers. Hooking her legs over his arms, he thrust into her without preamble, brutal and deep, not seeking to harm but to join. Desperate to make himself a part of her, to go so deeply inside her that she would never be free of him.

Rose didn't resist; she drove him on, matched his urgency with searing, welcoming heat. She met his thrusts, scored his skin to meat with nails and teeth, breath sobbing in her throat.

When their shared force tumbled them over, she rode him as mercilessly as he'd taken her, her cries of pleasure sharp as a banshee's wails. He held her hips with what he knew was a bruising grip and came, his sense of satisfaction coming as much from the relief of not having to restrain himself as from his orgasm. They didn't release. They wrested pleasure from each other and fell together, panting, bleeding, sore.

"You understand what it is like, don't you?" she asked. "To love someone so much you want to possess their very breath?"

He thought of the women he had cherished into their deaths. "That's it," he said. "That's it, exactly."

If he hadn't known before she was the one, he did now.

He insisted on bathing her with water he had brought, murmuring regret over his lack of restraint. No bruises marred her skin, which pleased him. He pressed his lips to where the warm living web of veins in her wrists and knees should be, feeling for the elusive rush of blood beneath the skin. That he found none should have bothered him, but strangely, it didn't. When at last he tried to kiss her, she turned her face from him.

"I have to know you're serious," she said. "I have to know you want to stay with me."

"Come away with me," he said, surprising himself. The steps of his courtships were even more rigid than those of his summoning rituals. He never asked until the third time, at the last. "Tomorrow."

Her eyes were enormous and dark. "You won't abandon me?"

"Never." He dragged in a deep breath and said the one thing he had never said to any of them while they were still alive to hear. "I love you, Rose."

She touched a finger to her lips, then his. "Tomorrow. Tomorrow, then forever."

He built a small fire in a brazier and opened his eastern window to the sun. Carefully, one by one, he burned each photograph, each beloved lock. With each small sacrifice, smoke puffed against his face, as if kissing him good-bye. He let them go, one by one. If Rose was to be before all others in his heart, he had to forsake all the others for her.

When he was finished, he lay on his bed and stared at the ceiling, willing the sun to die faster. Eventually, he slept.

He removed the scarf from his box; checked it with the care an anxious suitor would use to examine an engagement ring, smoothing and stroking the silk. The rose he had purchased was the most exquisite he could find, dark velvet petals and perfect hooked thorns. Everything must be flawless for Rose.

He showered and shaved, tamed his black hair with water and a comb. His suit was of the best tailoring, the white shirt beneath, though open at the throat, starched heavily enough to stand on its own. His stomach jittered as he prepared. He imagined it might be the way some men felt before their wedding, which this was, in a way, though far more binding. Weddings were as ephemeral as life. The ceremony of death would be what bound him to his Rose, not parted them.

When moonrise came, he took his gifts to the edge of the water, beside the willow tree. He found her huddled against the great trunk, legs tucked beneath her petticoat, turning a red-stained rock over in her hand. A bright wound gleamed at her temple. Ribbons of blood wove through her pale hair. She looked like a painting on dark velvet; two-dimensional, as if she were waning along with the moon. He felt no shock at the sight. No one so perfect for him could possibly be mortal. Without a word, he sat down beside her and waited.

"I've relived my death every full moon," she said. "Over a century now, it's been. William killed me for love and they hung him for it. What justice did that do me? I was still condemned to be a ghost, to keep reliving my last days all alone. If you say you'll love someone forever, you should stay with her, don't you think?"

"Yes," he said. He felt calm. More than calm. Peaceful. Saved. "You won't be alone anymore, Rose. Neither of us will."

She dropped the rock and stood before him, her demeanor as shy as a bride's as she laid her camisole and petticoat aside. He let her undress him, piece by piece. When she was finished, she knelt before him and caressed him until his cock rose, heavy and eager. He closed his eyes as she kissed it in benediction. Taking his hand, she led him into the water. The surface churned a little as she stepped in, the blood staining the froth. Aphrodite's ghost, returning to the place of her birth, he thought. The rose and garrote lay like forgotten wedding favors on the bank behind them.

Her lips brushed his. Cold. Fragile. He kissed her deeply, tasting anise, smelling myrrh. She drew him down to her. When they joined, he could no longer tell where she stopped and he began.

"Come away with me," Rose whispered, and drew his last breath from him in a long, sweet draught.

Inspired by the murder ballads "Down in the Willow Garden" and "Where the Wild Roses Grow."

THE BLOOD MOON KISS

Mitzi Szereto

Savannah, Georgia

The branches of a weeping willow caress the dark grass as gently as a lover's fingers. The artificially enhanced moonlight above illuminates the leaves with a silvery cast that's almost ghostlike as Christine moves into place, the cool night mist swirling around her bare feet and ankles. She's wearing only a nightgown, knee-length, pristine white, the fabric so gossamer that little is left to the observer's imagination. She's naked beneath it.

"Action!" shouts Mark Gaitzberger, director of "The Blood Moon Kiss."

Strong male fingers reach out from behind, seizing Christine's long black hair and pulling her head back to expose the vulnerable flesh of her neck. An arm appears from the same direction, fitting her waist into its vise. Her nipples stiffen as she feels a hot mouth fastening onto her jugular, followed by the pricking of sharp teeth. At that moment she experiences the shimmering of an orgasm, which begins at her neck and moves down her body, exploding into a thousand fragments of pleasure at her groin. If not for the arm encircling her waist, she would have collapsed to the ground. The bodice of her gown darkens as wetness streams from her neck. She doesn't need to look to know it will be red. How did it come to this?

Six Weeks Earlier
When you live in a place like Georgia and you get a call from your agent telling you he's just landed you a part in a hit television series that's being shot in Savannah—*and* you don't even have to audition for it, you aren't about to argue. I mean, let's get real: Georgia isn't exactly Hollywood. And for a Southern gal like me, this is home. Despite having no blood ties, I feel rooted here, a product of the soil like a Georgia peach. It's hard to explain, but something holds me here; maybe I was a Southern belle in a previous life, living on a big plantation and drinking mint juleps all day until some Rhett Butler turned up on my doorstep to ravish me. I just know that I don't want to be anywhere else, even if it means I'd stand a better chance at hitting the big time if I left. I'm happy enough to get the occasional role in a play at the Actor's Express Theater in Atlanta or in a TV commercial. By the way, that was me in the ad for Billy Bob's Burger Emporium. I was the waitress on the roller skates. You know, the one with the big beehive hairdo balancing the huge tray of food. I nearly twisted an ankle in those goddamned skates. I guess some things are better left in childhood.

I did wonder about the audition issue. It's practically unheard of to hire an actor without having that actor read for the part or do a screen test (unless maybe they're Johnny Depp or Angelina Jolie), but as they say, don't look a gift horse in the mouth. I've seen several episodes of the show and have to admit it's pretty good, as prime-time soap operas featuring a bunch of vampires go; I could do a lot worse. I also have to admit that one of the actors in it is really hot, and the thought of working with him gets me really hot as well. Not too professional, I know, but there you go. Not that I expect anything will happen—the guy's like the biggest heartthrob on television; he probably has women (and maybe even a few men) throwing themselves at his feet on a daily basis. Fred, that's my agent, said the series' producer had seen me on a public service ad for a battered women's shelter; I'd done this sort of one-woman performance deal, speaking directly to the camera as a wife who'd run away from her abusive husband. I realize it's only a TV commercial, but I'm proud of my work on it. I think I managed to portray just the right amount of fear and anguish. It was probably the fear component that got the producer's attention. Whatever, I'll be earning more money than I've ever earned in my life. By the time my stint is finished, I should be able to put a nice down payment on a house and maybe get a new car, too. Not bad for a few weeks' work.

Savannah
The night I first arrived on the set, seeing him for the first time...the entire planet seemed to shift. I was told in advance that most of the shooting would be done at night, so I'd already begun to prepare by sleeping during the day, practically living the life of a vampire before I'd stepped foot in Savannah. I'd met pretty much everyone in the cast and crew before I did my debut episode—well, everyone except the one person I most wanted to meet. I don't want to sound like some starry-eyed teenager here; I mean, we're all professionals, peers, and it's been a long time since I was a teenager, but I felt as if my heart would go bursting out of my rib cage, that's how excited I was to finally meet him.

Talen Dashkovar. God, even his name is enough to give you goose bumps.

We never got a chance to rehearse together before we came face-to-face for the first time. They'd used a stand-in for him, since he felt our debut scene would be much more powerful if we hadn't met yet. Apparently Talen's one of those method-actor types who actually becomes the character he's playing, and being as popular as he is, no one's inclined to disagree with him. I also heard some of the crew saying that he was feeling slightly under the weather (*again*) and resting up for the shoot. Judging from last season's episodes, he did seem to have a rather fragile quality beneath the boyish masculinity, though that might've been down to his pale complexion, which I'd assumed was enhanced by makeup so that he looked more vampiric. I already knew from the script that I too, would become paler with each episode, indicating that my life was slowly ebbing away, along with the blood in my veins. With my naturally black hair, the contrast of my skin would be made even more dramatic.

Our debut scene was brief, though that didn't lessen its impact. My character and his character share one of those fleeting-glance moments, full of lust and desire and the promise of more to come. It's late at night and Meridian (me) is walking past the fountain in a deserted Lafayette Square when Kyle (Talen) suddenly appears from the opposite direction. We both come to an abrupt stop, our figures illuminated by a full moon (with some added help courtesy of the lighting guys). Our eyes meet and hold; his are green and staggeringly beautiful, at times almost iridescent. I've never seen eyes like his before, not even on a cat, and they're not enhanced by any form of trickery from the makeup department or wizardry from special effects either.

Meridian is unable to move, she's so spellbound by him. After about a minute, Kyle smiles ever so slightly and steps aside, allowing her to pass. She awakens as if from a trance and glances around in confusion. Kyle has vanished from the square. A slow pan of the area reveals Meridian's lone figure standing by the fountain looking lost.

And Meridian *is* lost. Just as I am lost.

It's difficult to tell where he's from. His accent is like no other accent I've heard. At times it sounds Southern, then a moment later it sounds European, but it's always cultured, no matter which way it swings. My Southern accent has been beaten out of me by years of acting classes, leaving behind a generic North American one, which I can adapt at will, depending on what part I play. But Talen's a mystery. It's as if he came from out of nowhere and suddenly landed smack dab in the middle of a hit TV series. Before I left for Savannah, I tried to find out what I could about him from the Internet, but most of what came up was information related to the show, including some video interviews of him with other cast members. He always seemed to speak only if he had something of relevance to say, as though measuring each word's importance before uttering it, whereas his costars jabbered away with a youthful ebullience they apparently hadn't yet grown out of.

So when Talen invited me out for a drink on the first Sunday evening we had off since we started filming, I probably answered much too quickly. His mouth quirked up in one corner with what I came to associate as his trademark smile, as he named a popular place on River Street that overlooked the Savannah River. Apparently it used to be a cotton warehouse and was considered a place of historical interest, but one that served booze. I admit I dressed with a lot of care for the occasion, wanting to be sexy in an understated classy way—simple black dress, knee-length, bare legs, strappy sandals, lacy bra and panties, the latter of which I rarely wore (the lacy kind) since I generally had no occasion to, not being that big on dating. I guess it's safe to say I'm a loner—no surprise, considering my background. I'm not sure what I expected to happen between us, but the fact that *something* was happening between us was pretty obvious.

He was waiting by the bar, dressed casually in jeans and a long-sleeved black shirt, which had a couple of buttons undone at the top, revealing a discreet gold chain along with a tantalizing hint of smooth flesh like polished ivory. I wondered if the rest of him was as smooth and unmarred, since it looked doubtful he frequented the beach or tanning salon—at least not while playing the part of Kyle anyway. We greeted each other with a touching of hands, followed by a light kiss on the lips, which almost sent me reeling backward as if a current of electricity had been shot through me, though I managed to recover in time. "You're looking very lovely tonight, Christine," he said, his eyes looking more iridescent than I remembered. I nodded, unable to speak. He gestured to the bartender, and a moment later a glass of chilled white wine was placed before me. Whether I'd actually ordered it I can't say, but it is my drink of choice. How Talen could have known this I've no idea.

After a few nervous sips, I found myself talking all about my life, from my lonely childhood with foster parents who cared only for each other to my very first lover, who cared only for himself—a selfish young man I'd met at college who abandoned me when we thought I might be pregnant. I couldn't believe I was revealing so much about myself; it's not like me to open up to people, especially someone I barely know. Talen listened attentively and with appropriate sympathy, though he offered no private revelations of his own. I suppose I could have asked, but somehow it felt intrusive to do so.

No sooner had I finished my wine than another was put before me, and for Talen a glass of absinthe, for which the bartender performed that whole spoon and sugar-cube thing. I'd never tried it before, and Talen offered me a taste. I found it pretty vile, although he assured me I'd soon get used to it. I thought that a rather strange thing to say, but then Talen was... well...*strange*.

Sometime afterward I recall being in the backseat of a taxi, pressed close to him as the night flew past outside the car's windows. Then suddenly we were on a deserted beach among the sand dunes, the moonlight sparkling blue-white diamonds on the Atlantic, the scent of salt in my nostrils and the taste of it on my lips. It tasted like blood.

Her dress lies in a dark puddle on the white sand as she stands naked on the beach, facing away from him toward the watery horizon. His head is bowed into her neck, his arm crossed over her breasts, holding her firm against his chest. The nail of his thumb flicks against one nipple until it can harden no further, at which point he takes it between the pads of his thumb and index finger, pinching it lightly, then less so, varying the pressure so that she doesn't know what to expect, stopping just short of causing actual pain. She feels herself growing wet, so wet that it reaches her inner thighs, and she adjusts her stance, parting her legs to keep them from sticking together. The sand has retained the heat of the sleeping sun, and it feels warm and comforting against the bare soles of her feet. The moonlight makes her pale flesh look even more so, though with a blue tint that gives her an ethereal quality, like that of a ghostly angel. His hand leaves her breast to locate the V where her thighs meet. With a pairing of fingers he parts her folds, exposing the intimate pink to the sea air. The shock of what he's just done stops her from breathing. Her response is internal, all yearning thoughts and flowing juices. There's no movement from either of them, save for the gentle suction of his lips on her neck and the rhythmic sound of the ocean lapping the shore. The progress of the moon across the dark sky is the only thing that alerts her to the fact that time is passing.

They remain two silent figures on the beach, frozen in time and space, one fully clothed, the other exposed and vulnerable in her nudity. His fingers continue to hold her open, though he makes no move to stimulate her. It's as if he's tormenting her or displaying her secrets to some unseen observer—some nocturnal Peeping Tom who got lucky tonight and, rather than spying on a pair of teenagers going at it with unpracticed haste and little in the way of finesse, instead finds himself being treated to the sight of a man offering a detailed exhibition of a woman's genitals. Through half-lidded eyes she looks around, expecting to see a figure crouching in the tall grass of the dunes. But there's no one, no one on the beach but them. For a moment she feels almost disappointed.

A breeze off the ocean kisses her exposed flesh, as if drawing attention to her wetness. It's bubbling from her now, frothing hot and needy. The sea mist licks at her like a tongue, licking that place the man holding her has forced into exposure. And when she comes, she weeps from the force of it.

They lie together in a small clearing in the woods, chest on chest, pelvis on pelvis. The camera moves in on them as Kyle dips his head to drink from Meridian's neck, his left hand tenderly caressing her face and hair as if he's making love to her rather than placing her at risk of being transported from one of the living to one of the dead. Meridian moans with what sounds like orgasmic pleasure, and her hands reach up to Kyle's head, her fingers twining in his dark hair. There's a brief moment when they tighten their grip and actually pull, though this moment quickly passes, making the observer wonder if it was ever there at all. The camera lens does not pick up on the fact that Talen's other hand has slipped between their two pelvises, or that his middle finger is wedged deeply inside her.

"Cut!" shouts the director.

Neither Talen nor Christine moves. He continues to lie on top of her, his face buried in her neck, his heart pounding hard against hers. Although Christine's eyes are closed, her lips quirk upward into a tiny smile, as if she holds a secret.

The crew collects their gear and moves off, chuckling among themselves good-naturedly at an on-camera romance that has obviously moved off-camera. *Best of luck to them,* they think, having seen their fair share of such things over the years. Christine and Talen make a striking couple. In fact, they look as if they're destined to be together. Why *shouldn't* they hook up?

When the echoes of voices can no longer be heard, Talen leaves Christine's neck and positions himself at her knees, where he draws up the hem of her dress, his earlier explorations having told him that she has forgone wearing panties tonight. He does so slowly, torturously, allowing Christine to experience the erotic shock of being fully exposed to him. The wounds on her neck bubble slightly with blood, but he has only drunk a small amount, all too aware that he's pulling her nearer and nearer to the life he has led for the last century and a half. She's almost ready to make the transition.

When the hem finally reaches her waist, Talen bends her legs at the knees and pushes her thighs apart, lowering his face to the portion of her that he has brought into exposure. Her positioning forces the lips of her sex to distend outward and he places his own before them, meeting their humid kiss. The taste and scent of her is such that he feels in danger of losing control and he stabs his tongue inside her, the tightness enveloping it promising a pleasure so exquisite he fears he might not be able to wait for much longer. But wait he must.

Each thrust of Talen's tongue is met by a return thrust from Christine. She wants him inside her so badly; she cannot understand why he's making her wait. But the question's soon forgotten as Talen's tongue changes tack, applying dizzying swirls and circuits around her inner lips, teasing and tormenting and flicking over the flesh at the center. A warm shimmering begins to move along her body, starting both at the top of her head and the tips of her toes and traveling steadily toward her middle, sending electrical currents through every pore and hair follicle. These are no ordinary sensations, no ordinary precursors to the final moment of pleasure, and suddenly she can't breathe. She wonders if this might be it; that this time she really will die.

Christine has felt the breath of death before. It happens each time Talen drinks from her—that acceleration of the heartbeat followed by a curious awareness of things she never noticed: the rustle of insects in the grass, the distant sound of a bird's wings flapping in flight, occasionally even human voices murmuring in languages she can't recognize. His feeding on her has become more and more indistinguishable from her sexual pleasure, and she always believes she won't survive it—that it will finally be *the last time.*

The sound of Christine's wetness is amplified to her ears, and she pushes her pelvis into Talen's face, silently begging him to continue. She loves the sound of him licking her and wants it to go on forever. He seems to share her desire and never once falters; it's as if his tongue is memorizing her intimate terrain or perhaps even reacquainting itself with it after a too-long absence. When Christine's orgasm is at last brought to fruition by his tongue, she's pulled from this world and transported into another.

Afterward Talen rises up from between Christine's thighs, his lips shining with her moisture. As he looks down at her, he licks it away, his eyes burning in the night like emeralds that have been set on fire.

I have to smile whenever I look in the mirror and see the bruise on my neck with the two matching puncture marks located in the center. I touch the area carefully, though it isn't sore. Touching it gives me pleasure, as though the wound retains a memory of the orgasms I experience when the blood's being drawn from it. Not for the first time, I wonder why no one seems to have noticed anything unusual. There have been less and less instances of makeup having to come in and apply fake blood to my neck and any other parts of me it's spilled onto. Didn't they ever wonder where it was coming from? Or was the reality so unbelievable that their minds shut down until they neither saw nor realized what was in front of them? Do I even believe it myself?

Though it's been less than a month since I joined the cast, I know that I'm in love with Kyle. Or rather *Talen*. I get the two mixed up sometimes. Playing a character, particularly that of a woman who believes that spending an eternity as one of the undead is a better option than knowing she'll eventually lose her beloved by the fault of her own mortality is not exactly an idea I can't relate to. Having said that, I've never had such thoughts about other men. Envisioning myself with someone several months down the line, or even years, was as far as I'd ever managed. But eternity? No. I can safely say I've never entertained such a concept or loved anyone enough to desire it. Until now. I wonder if I'm mad, or if Talen is mad. Though if we are, then I'm happy to exist in madness with him, even if it means it might eventually kill me. If his artistic perfectionism has actually led him to become the person he's playing, so be it. Or perhaps it was him all along....

He knows I want him inside me. Want it so badly that yes, I'm willing to die for it, to let him take away what remains of my life, just like Meridian. But he's in control. There's nothing I can say or do; if or *when* it happens, it will be his decision. So I wait. Patiently.

And at last I get my wish.

It's 2:00 a.m. on a Sunday morning when Talen takes me to the Bonaventure Cemetery. Although not the first choice on most couples' lists for romantic destinations, it feels right that we should go there—that it should be in this place where we consummate our relationship, at least in the Biblical sense. I feel no fear being here among the dead. They don't wish me harm.

Like a fine Southern gentleman, Talen takes my arm and guides me through the darkness toward the oldest part of the cemetery. We eventually arrive at a moss-draped oak that overhangs a large gray tombstone. Despite its age, it looks surprisingly well tended, and I notice that a bouquet of flowers has recently been placed at the grave. He indicates with a nod for me to lower myself onto the grass. The blades feel cool and welcoming-soft beneath the thin fabric of my dress and I lie back as if I'm in my own bed, stretching my arms above and behind me to create a pillow for my head. I smile up at him with a trust I've never given anyone.

Talen kneels down beside me, pulling my dress up over my thighs, my belly, my breasts, and then over my head. I'm naked beneath it. I only wear dresses when I'm with him, never jeans or anything constricting, and generally no underclothes, not even if he and I are shooting a scene. Ever since the first time we were together, that dream-night on the beach, I've stopped wearing anything beneath my dresses. I want to be available for him at all times, should he desire a touch, a taste, a scent. Sometimes he'll just pull me into his face and breathe me in, not touching me. Even this makes me come.

He leans down and kisses my lips, his tongue licking the top one, then the bottom, before sliding into my mouth to meet mine. His saliva is like a fine wine and I sip it from his tongue, savoring its herbal sweetness. I could spend hours like this, but when Talen breaks our kiss to straddle my chest, I suspect he has other plans. His fingers unzip the fly of his jeans and I open my mouth, pleased to be given still more of him to savor. The moment my tongue makes contact with the flesh being offered my body begins tingling with that electrical current I always experience from his contact. I can actually hear it buzzing in my ears, as if a million bees are swarming around my head. I taste his tangy-sweetness and moisture fills my eyes. How can it be possible to love someone this much? Talen allows me a few minutes to indulge myself, and I lick and suck at him hungrily as bits of moss from the overhanging branch of the old oak drop greenish-gray tears onto my nakedness. Then he decides I've had enough. On this occasion my mouth will not be receiving the completion of his pleasure.

There's no preamble, no courteousness, as he jerks open my thighs and enters me with one thrust. His lips swoop down and fasten onto my neck, his teeth breaking through the fragile skin they have broken through so many times before. I arch my pelvis upward, swallowing him so deeply that it feels as if he's entered my womb. For a moment I allow myself to wonder what kind of child we'd have—would it be human, or would it be like...*him?*

The soft suckling sounds at my neck as he drinks from me cause my heart to swell with tenderness, and I cradle his head against me, stroking his dark hair and placing little kisses anywhere my lips can reach. It's as though I'm breastfeeding my child, giving it nourishment to allow it to live. Then I realize that yes, this is exactly what I'm doing, only Talen is not my child; he's my lover. He moves inside me with short hard thrusts that continue to increase in speed and violence, alerting me to his impending climax. As his pelvis grinds against mine, the steel of his zipper occasionally catches in my pubic hair or bites into the surrounding flesh. I welcome the pain; it's just one more element of the pleasure he gives me. I look up at the moss-draped oak and see an owl observing us with its large saucer eyes, as if it understands exactly what we're doing.

My hands leave Talen's head and slip beneath the seat of his jeans, fastening onto a buttock each. They are smooth and warm, and I allow my fingertips to skirt the crease, which is hot and humid and unexpectedly inviting. I can tell he's nearly there; the sucking at my neck has become more frantic, as have his strokes. Suddenly my breath catches as I feel molten lava shooting into me, filling me until I'm overflowing, pooling beneath me on the grass in a boiling puddle. As I imagine it soaking into the dark rich earth, deeper and deeper, until it reaches whoever lies beneath us, I cry out, consumed by an ecstasy that surpasses any I've yet experienced. With a loud flap of wings the owl takes off. The ground beneath me vanishes and I'm lifted up into the black Savannah sky. I too, have become a creature of flight, swooping on the currents and playing tag with the stars, my cries of pleasure like the keening of a bird of prey. Talen is with me, our feathered fingers entwined, offering a reassuring touch of safety in this strange environment. I know that he won't let anything happen to me; I'm safe with him. I will always be safe with him.

My eyes open and I'm lying on the grass by the oak tree. Talen's beside me, still exposed, the beautiful length of him glistening from our combined wetness. We're holding hands, our breathing perfectly matched, as if we share the same set of lungs. I prop myself up on one arm so that I can look into his eyes. They're completely iridescent now, and I feel myself being bathed in a green fire. "I love you," I say.

Talen studies me with a serious expression, and several moments pass before he finally responds. "But do you love me enough?"

The sky is starting to lighten, indicating that it will soon be daylight. Neither of us has slept, and we have another long night of work ahead. The filming of "The Blood Moon Kiss" will soon be reaching an end, at least for this season, and I've no idea whether I'll be invited back for the next—or if there will even *be* a next. Talen helps me up from the ground and brushes the errant bits of grass from my dress. I laugh a girlish laugh, finding his gesture sweetly familial. This is when I notice what's been carved into the headstone at the place of our lovemaking.

TALEN DASHKOVAR
BORN MAY 3, 1824
DIED DECEMBER 1, 1853

Before this fully registers in my consciousness, I note another inscription directly below it.

BELOVED WIFE
ADELINA DASHKOVAR
BORN MARCH 17, 1817
DIED NOVEMBER 28, 1853

He reaches up behind his neck to unclasp the gold chain he always wears. That's when I notice for the first time the locket that hangs from it. I can't recall ever seeing a man wearing a locket before, but then, Talen isn't like other men. He clicks it open and places it on my palm with great care. "Adelina," he says softly. "My wife."

A tiny black-and-white photograph of a young woman looks up at me. Her features are dramatic, the hair and eyes intensely dark against a face nearly the white of snow. There's something familiar about her, but I can't at the moment place it. "She died carrying our child." Talen's eyes glitter like minute shards of green glass. A few slide down his cheeks and he turns away, his face crumpling.

I take his hand and press it to my cheek, his heartbreak so palpable that I feel my own heart breaking as well.

Later that day while brushing my teeth before the mirror at the bathroom sink, I suddenly realize why Adelina seemed so familiar. The face inside Talen's locket is the same face that looks out at me from the mirror.

"The minute I saw you on that television commercial, even with the ridiculous beehive hairdo I recognized you." Talen smiles, the tiny lines at his eyes crinkling with affection. "I'd know my Adelina anywhere."

Talen's convinced I'm the reembodiment of his dead wife. He's even admitted that he used some kind of mind control ability he has to influence the show's producer to get me hired for the role of Meridian. So much for my Emmy Award–winning performance as a roller-skating waitress at a drive-in burger joint.

I've never really given much thought to reincarnation. As a concept it has its appeal; I mean, the idea of never being truly dead, of having a second chance at life, or a third, or a fourth...who *wouldn't* want that? The fact that I know absolutely nothing about where I come from, or from whom, lends Talen's theory even more credence. I was a Jane Doe, a baby abandoned at birth, then later placed with foster parents. My past is a blank sheet of paper. Now Talen is filling it in, only with facts from a very distant past—facts that resound deep within me like an iron bell being hit by a hammer, making my acceptance of the impossible possible. For the first time in my life, things are making sense.

He grabs my hands and presses them to his heart, which beats hard and strong beneath his shirt. "I've looked for you everywhere. I never stopped looking, not for a single moment in the century and a half since you left me."

It's beyond my comprehension to be loved by a man to such a degree that he would look for me for more than 150 years. To be honest, I can't imagine *any* of the men I've been involved with even going to the trouble of walking around the block to look for me.

Adelina had died before Talen had been given a chance to transition her. They'd agreed that she would not relinquish her "normal" life until they'd started a family, believing it fairer on the children to decide for themselves whether they wished to change over. Of course, neither Talen nor Adelina knew if having one normal parent and one vampire parent would result in a vampire child, but they still felt the decision should remain with their future children, if such a decision would, in fact, be theirs to make. However, the couple hadn't reckoned on

Adelina dying—and taking with her their unborn child, who'd been growing outside the womb. Talen had railed against the world, cursing everyone in it for killing the only thing that ever mattered to him, the only thing he loved. Adelina.

"I guess there were a lot of things I didn't know back then," says Talen, "such as the fact that vampires can't kill themselves by flinging themselves in front of a speeding carriage drawn by a team of horses." He laughs at this, but his mirth sounds hollow. "Clearly, I looked dead, or at least dead enough to be buried."

The conversation is surreal. But then, everything that's happened since I came to Savannah has been surreal. Even more surreal is the fact that Adelina died from an ectopic pregnancy. It had turned out that I'd been correct when I thought I was pregnant in college. My boyfriend took off, and a few weeks later abdominal pain and bleeding landed me in the emergency ward, where I was diagnosed with a tubal pregnancy. By then the fetus was dead. As I tell all this to Talen, he breaks down into sobs. "I can't bear to think I might've lost you before I'd even found you again!"

The following evening just before they are to be driven into the Georgia countryside for their final shoot, Talen takes Christine aside to once again show her the locket. This time when he clicks it open, she sees not Adelina as she was in the 1850s, but Adelina as she would be in the twenty-first century. Suddenly Christine realizes that the photo inside the locket is of *her* and she smiles.

And Talen knows that it's time to ask the question he's been waiting to ask.

Meridian lies on the ground looking up at Kyle, his lips shiny-red with her blood in the artificially enhanced moonlight. It's a pivotal scene and the last one in the season, and the powers that be have left its filming till the very end rather than shooting out of sequence. They don't realize that the decision has not been entirely theirs, and that other powers have influenced the decision as well. It's the scene in which Meridian acquiesces to being turned into a vampire by Kyle so that she can be with him for eternity. He hasn't forced her or exerted any form of mind control on her; she offers herself of her own free will and with the full realization that there's no returning to what she was, no going back. *Ever.*

Epilogue

> Actress Collapses on Set of Hit TV Series
> —*USA Today*

> SAVANNAH, GA — Cast and crew of the hit vampire TV series "The Blood Moon Kiss" were stunned yesterday on the final day of filming by the sudden collapse of actress Christine Emberson.
> Emberson, 36, who plays Meridian in the popular prime-time vampire soap, had just finished shooting a night scene with actor Talen Dashkovar (who plays Kyle) when she collapsed. Paramedics were called to the scene, but by then the actress had recovered. She was later escorted off the set by Dashkovar.
> "Ms. Emberson has been suffering from exhaustion," said Mark Gaitzberger, the series' director. "It's not uncommon in a show like ours. We often work all night for several nights running. It was obvious to everyone that the schedule's been taking its toll on

her. What she needs is a good long rest."

Dashkovar, 29, who's in a relationship with the actress, apparently agrees. He has taken Emberson to his secluded retreat in the Blue Ridge Mountains until she's fully recovered. "I ask everyone to please respect our privacy," said heartthrob Dashkovar. "I must look after Christine. She's my priority now."

Neither Dashkovar nor Emberson has indicated whether they plan to return for the series' third season.

PAINTED

Anna Meadows

S he had once hung in the foyer, all gleaming oil paint on
stretched canvas. Mr. Lawrence had won her in a wager
with a friend, though he never would say how. Benjamin
had asked once or twice, when he came inside to replace the
hollyhocks and sweet peas in the vases. But Mr. Lawrence
would only clap a hand on his back and say, "The train
into Kewley is always late, m'boy." He'd then notice the dirt
his palm had garnered from Benjamin's shirt, and would
quietly brush it away, inspiring the young groundskeeper to
shrink toward the back door and mumble something about
the hydrangeas.

But when Mr. Lawrence married, his new wife made it clear
that the painting of the dark-haired woman would be the first
thing to go. "It's vulgar," she said, in the same breath as she
mentioned that the drapes could really use replacing. "She looks
like a tart." Each time she passed through the foyer, she cast
a critical eye on the lace that dipped low along the woman's

décolletage. To her, the woman's dress, red as currants full and shameless on the branch, was immodest, like a bared breast. The ruffle of petticoat peeking from the woman's skirts, which Benjamin drew in his head as he lay in bed each night, seemed as indecent as her unbound tresses. A woman had no right to take such indelicate joy in her own body, to be so smug in displaying her own form, and the new Mrs. Lawrence had no shyness in announcing as much when Benjamin replaced a bouquet of wilting alliums or the maid dusted the livery cupboard, whether or not they seemed to be listening. She'd even heard, while at the dressmaker's, that the Jenners' second-youngest daughter had kissed the stable groom the very evening she first saw the painting, but she wouldn't countenance such a story by repeating it.

The new Mrs. Lawrence might have mentioned it if she'd known that the Jenners' second-youngest daughter hadn't been the only one. The first night Mr. Lawrence had placed the painting, the maid had crept along the servants' corridor after eleven, and had barely gotten back to her own bed by sunup the next morning. She'd so startled Benjamin that he'd nearly dropped his armful of amaryllis. He steadied himself and let her pass, saying nothing of her wrinkled dress or undone hair, loose down her back like the painted woman's instead of tight in its usual chignon.

Later in the morning, the maid, her clothes pressed and hair newly arranged, dawdled in the foyer while Benjamin saw to the vases on the credenza. She always stole quick, barely noticeable glances at the painted woman while she cleaned, but this time she cast looks toward Benjamin. She was waiting for him to say whether or not he'd mention to Mr. Lawrence or his mother that he'd seen her coming from the cook's bedroom.

He said nothing and pretended he'd seen nothing. His silence seemed to satisfy her. She'd often seen the shiver that spread through his back when he looked at the painted woman for more than a few seconds, and she knew that if anyone were to understand her spell, it was Benjamin. She was a blaze of moon, and they were each seas she pulled into tides.

The maid had stopped in front of the frame. "Poor girl," she said.

"Why?" Benjamin asked, not looking up from the cut hydrangeas.

"She's just got to sit there that way," said the maid. "She can't do anything but look pretty."

He hadn't thought of it, and he brushed the idea away; he ached to look at her, and the possibility that she might not care to be looked upon irritated him like an oyster's grain of sand. But however much pity the maid held for the woman on the canvas, she admired her as much as the groundskeeper. She kept quiet during the younger Mrs. Lawrence's lectures about the painting, though her face blossomed with color each time, and she excused herself to see the cook about supper. She always returned with a ringlet escaped from her mobcap, smoothing fresh wrinkles out of her apron. The cook had infrequent cause to dally in the foyer, but Benjamin had once seen her wink at the woman in the painting as she passed, as though to thank her for offering the kindling to the maid's passions.

Mr. Lawrence's mother had long looked askance at the painted woman, and when her son married, she seconded his new bride's disapproval. "Really, Edmund," she said as she ascended the stairs with her evening cup of camellia-bergamot. "Isn't it about time you took it down?" She added, with a whisper, "You have a woman of your own now."

But it had never been about the woman. Benjamin knew that. Mr. Lawrence had never given her a good look. He hadn't memorized the mahogany of her hair, the soft olive of her face, or the shades of her dress, deep and varied as the roses that climbed the west garden wall. The only appreciation his employer had ever showed was to note the fine seascape in the background, as though the woman were invisible, or to examine the intricate winged heads of angels carved into the wood of the frame. Their frightful visages made Benjamin recoil, but if he looked past them to the honeyed apples of the painted woman's cheeks, she set his arousal on an edge so fine that the slightest touch would make him shudder like an anemone.

For Mr. Lawrence, the pride of the painting came in eliciting grumbles from Mr. Herman whenever he visited. But it couldn't have meant much to Mr. Herman either; he'd never asked for it back, and whenever he suggested they "go another round," he always had his eye on a crystal decanter, violet-brown with port wine, and never on the framed canvas. Neither had imagined what she might feel like up underneath her petticoats, like the inner velvet of dew-wet snapdragons, or new blooms of love-lies-bleeding, soaked with rain.

Benjamin's heart tightened at the possibility of her getting sold or tossed out, or returned to Mr. Herman, who hardly missed her. Neither of them knew the feeling of her reds and browns settling over him like a fever, the taint of dreaming about stripping the satin and silk down to the magnolia ivory of her slip. Benjamin almost spoke up to say he would keep the painting in his cottage at the back of the property if it would help. But he thought better and went back to adding fresh water to the vases.

He spent the night wondering what would become of her, his little sleep made restless with dreams of her vanishing like color underwater. But the next morning he found her propped up in a corner of the pantry. Though the muscles in his back tensed to think of her in the small, dark space, at least he could visit her, taking a little longer than he had to when he strung herbs to dry in the window.

But the next morning, Mr. Lawrence's wife found it, and her fit of screaming reached all the way to the groundskeeper's cottage, wrenching Benjamin awake. He dressed quickly and reached the house at the peak of her ranting.

"Get rid of it," she told her husband.

"What would you have me do with it?" Mr. Lawrence asked.

"Give it back," she said.

"I can't give it back," he said, his hearty laugh only enraging his wife further. "I won it. Herman will think I'm saying he was right."

"Then throw it out," she said. "Burn it."

The thought of seeing the woman in the painting torn or crumbled to ash overcame Benjamin. His nightly dreams of her tormented him like the sting and sugar of blackberry brambles, but the loss of her would leave his sleep barren as a pebbled shore.

Before he could reconsider, he was in the pantry doorway. "I could keep it for him, ma'am," he said. "Then you wouldn't have to look at it."

Every gaze found him. Mr. and Mrs. Lawrence. Mr. Lawrence's mother. The cook and the maid, whose disheveled hair and hurriedly broken embrace were unnoticed in the fray.

"I wouldn't mind," Benjamin said. "I've got the room."

They continued to stare, and he cringed.

Mr. Lawrence burst out with another full laugh, and everyone jumped. The ladies' hands flew to their hearts.

"Genius." Mr. Lawrence slapped Benjamin on the back so hard the young groundskeeper stumbled. "I'll bring old Herman by next time. He'll be pale as a turnip when he sees his little prize can't even find a place in the foyer."

His wife dismissed both him and Benjamin with a flick of her wrist. "Fine," she said. "As long as it's out of the house. I won't have it in the house."

Benjamin exhaled so long his stomach stung. He had saved her, and she would be water and wild roses to his midnight fields.

The woman was life-sized, and the painting so large that Mr. Lawrence insisted on helping him out across the grounds. "It would be a shame to see the frame chipped," he said. Once they leaned the painting against a wall inside the cottage, Mr. Lawrence blew the dust from his fingers. "She's fastidious, isn't she?" he said. "She's even talking about moving the credenza."

Benjamin only nodded.

"When are you going to get yourself a wife, Ben?" Mr. Lawrence asked.

"I hadn't much thought of it," said Benjamin.

"Smart boy," said Mr. Lawrence on his way out.

Benjamin wished the fruit trees didn't need pruning or the hedges trimming. For the first time, he could study the woman in the painting without worrying if Mr. Lawrence would offer him a speech on the fine gilt work along the frame, or if the elder Mrs. Lawrence would take the opportunity to ask if he wasn't perhaps overwatering the violas. He wanted to trace her fawn-brown features until he could imagine their warmth on his hands. If he lingered on her dress, the shape that the folds of rose and sangria only hinted at would turn him hard as a birch root. He craved her febrile stare that left him mired in agony.

But his patience was strong, built by years of watching saplings take root and waiting for the first crocuses to break through the snow in March. He pulled the milk thistles from the bulb beds, repaired a fencepost a fox had splintered, and replaced a cracked brick in the walkway. By late afternoon the clouds in the east tumbled and darkened, and he knew he'd better see to a branch that struck an upstairs bedroom window whenever the wind kicked up. When his thoughts strayed, he held her at a safe distance. As though the painted woman could hear his daydreams, he whispered assurances that his reveries would be hers alone once darkness and stars had spilled across the sky.

He raked the leaves last, because every hour there were more and he might as well clear as many as he could just before dusk. The ashes and beeches had burst into flame the week before, and the wind and intermittent rain stripped the ambers and reds from the branches and carpeted the grounds. He gathered them for mulch as more fell, a few catching in his hair or in the cuffs of his sleeves and boots. The wind threaded cold through his collar. The sky glowed lavender and pale blue with the approaching storm. He'd have twice as many leaves by morning.

When he'd finished his work, he washed his hands and face, as though the woman in the painting might see him. She might have been a Spanish princess, the Strait of Gibraltar in the background, or a Corsican noblewoman, the Mediterranean Sea offering her its iris blue. He could at least scrub the crescent moons of topsoil from under the whites of his fingernails.

He stood before her, arms crossed over his chest to steady himself against her gaze. He'd memorized every inch of her, and now he reviewed her again to test his memory. She was unlike the other portraits in the Lawrence house. She did not sit straight-backed in an upholstered chair or pose on an embroidered chaise in a dim parlor. Instead she lounged on a sunyellow stone terrace, resting against satin pillows heaped on a woven rug. Instead of pinned, her hair was loose; brown as the inner peels of black birch, it fell around her shoulders and gently obscured the shadow between her breasts. Her dress sloped into a soft V at the neckline, and the damask pooled around her legs as she reclined on the wool carpet. A faint smile and her left hand grasping at the fabric suggested she liked the feeling of half drowning in the silk and velvet. That floret of mirth allowed him to imagine, for a moment, that if she liked the looks of him she might let him do a few of the thousand things he'd imagined. Her right hand absentmindedly fiddled with the single strand of blush-colored seed pearls on her collarbone, and he couldn't help thinking where her hands might stray if he offered her his body.

Once he'd reviewed every curve and color, he tore his gaze from the fallow shade of her skin and the folds of her dress. He shouldn't spend the night staring at her. It would be an early morning; there would be leaves to clear from the roofs and gutters, and the storm would fell tree branches and ravage the perennials.

He dreamt of her anyway. He lay with her under the green ash trees, the torrents tearing their clothes away. His hands followed the contours of her breasts and hips like he was charting a map as soft and tea-stained as her skin. Her mouth found his shoulder, her teeth bearing gently into him as her tongue left wet sparks pulsing in his muscle. He swallowed a groan as she let him go and rested her lips against his neck. He found her wet as the inner petals of a camellia, where the last drops of a summer shower hid from the sun. They left each other ruined as blue lilacs in the night storm.

He woke just after midnight, straining to remember how she felt. He was left only with that familiar longing. Full raindrops struck the roof, but the storm couldn't have roused him and pulled him from her. He'd grown so used to the downpours and the scream of the wind that a bird's feet scratching along the shingles was more likely to stir him from sleep than rain or the thrashing of tree boughs. He sat up in bed, closing his eyes to make out a faint scratching sound. Not birds. They would never be out in this weather. Shutting his eyes tighter, he found its direction: the fence he'd had to repair three times since August. The fox was back, burrowing into the ground. If he scared it, it might scurry away before it wrecked another post.

He lit no lamps; he wanted his vision sharp in the dark. He pulled on trousers and tripped over a few soft things on the way to the door that must have been blankets fallen from the bed. He didn't stop to set them back in place; a few more moments, and the fox would have splintered another post and gone.

The rain soaked him as soon as he was in the open, and the wind whipped the droplets into sprays. Water stuck his shirt and trousers to his body and pasted locks of hair to his forehead. He was already drenched, and didn't bother shielding himself as he walked along the fence and the garden wall. The moon had lit up the clouds, the glow guiding his way. Every piece seemed in order. The ground was dark with mud, but he couldn't find any patches the fox had dug up, or holes made by raccoons or rabbits. He'd imagined the sound and had nothing but dripping clothes to show for his efforts.

He returned to the little house and lit a lamp, his boots squelching with every step. Rain had sealed the longest pieces of his hair to the nape of his neck, letting a ribbon of water down the knobs of his spine. He was grateful for how it cooled and calmed his wanting.

He stripped off his shirt, draping it to dry on the back of a chair as his eyes adjusted to the light. Dark shapes cluttered the floor. He blinked a few more times to make them out. He hadn't tripped over his bedcovers on the way to the door; there were pillows there, each made of satin striped crimson and burgundy. A woven rug slouched in the corner, and great swathes of fringed fabric pooled around the pillows.

They couldn't have belonged to the ladies of the house. Both the elder Mrs. Lawrence and the younger would have dismissed them as too showy or exotic. They hardly seemed like anything Mr. Lawrence might have owned, though perhaps he had also won them from another betting friend, and thought Benjamin's cottage a good place for all things to which his new wife might object. But who would have brought them, and when? Benjamin always locked the door at night, and surely he would have woken to anyone trying to get in. Had that been the noise he'd heard earlier?

He piled the pillows in the corner, rolled the rug, and folded the fabric, which must have once been curtains; he'd ask Mr. Lawrence in the morning.

Though his trousers and undershirt were soaked, his hair disarrayed, he cast a last look toward the woman in the painting and gave a nod of goodnight.

But the woman was not there. In her place was another painting of the same size.

The frame was the same, carved with those terrible winged heads. The woman, and all her damask and velvet, were gone. In her place was a sprawling blue sea beneath a teal sky, with the band of a marble terrace along the bottom of the picture, as though showing where the artist might have been.

Had someone switched the paintings and stolen the original? Was this another of Mr. Lawrence's jokes? Had Mrs. Lawrence changed her mind and made good on her threat to burn the picture?

Benjamin sank to the edge of his bed, not caring that the seat of his trousers would dampen the blanket. He rested his elbows on his knees, his forehead in his palms. Either they'd taken her, or they'd think he had, and he wouldn't know until morning.

He shifted his weight, and caught the flash of satin out of the corner of his eye. A woman's dress was draped on the chair by the window. Mr. Lawrence must have been having a joke. Any moment he would jump from the closet and frighten Benjamin out of his skin.

It was too young for Mr. Lawrence's mother and the neckline too low for his wife's tastes. The fabric caught the light in a half dozen shades of blush and red. Just as the damask and velvet stirred his memory, he realized someone was behind him. He thought for a moment it might be Mr. Lawrence, ready to reap the fruit of his joke. But Benjamin could feel the shadow of the intruder's heat, a shape too small to be his employer's. Had he left the cottage door unlocked while he was out?

He turned, as slowly as he could, as though giving the intruder time to flee through a window. He jumped to his feet at the sight of the woman in his bed.

She didn't return his startled expression. She only moved her legs under the blanket and let her dark hair fall in front of her eyes. Her curls, almost pulled straight by the weight of her mane, were dry, as were her skin and what little clothing she wore. How could she have gotten in and not have gotten soaked?

His back was pressed to the opposite wall, and he still couldn't move. She looked young, around his age, though she could have been older, the hint of mischief in her eyes accounting for her look of youth. Her shoulders were bare, a corset's cream lace holding her breasts, and the blanket draped around her hips. Before he could resist the thought, he could almost feel the gentle sway of her hair and dress on his skin, not yet venturing to imagine the scent of her.

He looked back at the things scattered around the cottage—the seascape, which looked almost the same as the background of the original painting; the scarlet fabric and pillows that seemed to have tumbled from inside the canvas; the dress on the chair, with its shades of fall-fire satin. And the woman in his bed, with her kohl-black eyebrows and lashes and the red tulip of her mouth, and the yearning he knew as well as the rhythm of his own breathing.

He shook his head to clear the thought. He hadn't eaten anything strange or had anything to drink. He couldn't recall having struck his head. He put a hand to his own forehead, but it was no warmer than usual, not enough to bring on a waking fever dream. She bit her lip and beckoned to him, and his body obeyed before he had a moment to consider.

The moment he touched her, he hungered to touch all of her. His hands could not move fast enough. His fingers wouldn't pause long enough to map her before exploring the next curve or vale of her form. His patience had left him. She had woven it into more passion than his body could hold.

Desire ignited his cells and lit up his veins like threads of moon, hot and yellow-gold on the horizon. She pulled him into his own bed as though it were hers, unfastening his trousers. Her hurried fingers thwarted her. He hardened against her palms as she worked at each button, only the thin layers of fabric keeping her fingers from him. The closer she came to touching him, the less he thought he could wait. But she was in no hurry; toying with his clothes and making him wait delighted her. He recaptured his patience and let her.

She peeled his undershirt from his torso and kissed him so roughly he shuddered, her lips warm and alive. He dared to put his hands on her waist, and the lace of her corset pressed back against his palms. Her skin let off the scent of cloves and cinnamon. She laughed like a shimmer of rain as she ruffled his damp hair and feathered her fingers over his crotch, his nerves so bright and sensitive he blushed and slouched away. When she saw his shyness, she crawled onto him and pushed him against the bed. His back hit the mattress and she pinned him down. Her lips barely grazing his grew his ache until it neared pain. He turned his head, resting his still-damp cheek against the bed, and tried to hide behind the wet locks of his hair.

But she wouldn't let him go. Her hair fell like dark water on his neck. She watched him just long enough to catch his gaze and give him her smile before she sealed her lips against his. Her kiss emboldened him, and his hands slowly strayed from his sides to the curves of her breasts and the ribbons of her garters. He untied the strips of deep red satin and eased the lace bands down her thighs and knees. She straddled him, her bare legs holding him, and tore away his underclothes.

When he realized she had him completely naked, he felt sheepish and tricked, but she didn't resist when he pulled at the lacing of her corset. She laughed softly, moving to try to help him. She could not stay still, and her restlessness both aroused him and tormented him, hindering his first efforts to undress her.

He did not unlace her like she had unbuttoned him; he slowed himself down, loosened one pair of ribbon loops at a time. She still wriggled. It occurred to him that the maid might have been right; she might have felt trapped inside the canvas, frozen in the demure mischief of her painted posture. She had wanted to move. She wanted not only sex; she wanted to bend her back and stretch her soft limbs. She hungered for the feel of his skin and the sheets and the cool air against her bare skin. Had she been imprisoned in the portrait? Could he now hold her and keep her?

He freed her from the last scrap of lace, and the sight of her unrestrained breasts took the last of his shyness and left longing in its place. Her hair tangled and flooded him with the perfume of oranges. He gently parted her thighs, and she invited him in, letting him turn her soft laughs to gasps and sudden inhalations. He moved into her, their bodies building a slow, deep rhythm, and she tipped the bowl of her hips to open herself. When a scream welled up inside her, he felt her hold it back. He pressed his mouth to hers so she could unloose the sound into his mouth. The warmth of his tongue took the last of her restraint. Her cry shimmered past his lips and met his voice as it wavered at the back of his throat.

With every stroke of her fingers, she painted his chaste body into life, until he thought she might be pulling him into the painting with her, to the sunlit marble and red satin of her terrace. If she'd come seeking a companion, he was happy to be taken and made hers. The darkness hid their greed for each other's bodies; the rain and peals of thunder muffled her surprised shrieks of pleasure and the low sounds he held at the back of his throat.

She felt him tremble, resisting his body's release, and she wrapped her legs around him and dug her heels into his back. The sudden feeling of being forced closer to her, being forced a little farther inside her, broke his hesitation. She'd enveloped him in her soft darkness, hot and sweet as the syrup of maidenhair ferns. She held his desire prisoner in the peony petals between her thighs. His pleasure finished as her cry bloomed against his mouth. She lifted her hips to receive it, eager to let it mingle with her wetness; he took the small of her back in his hands to help her. It was the last moment he felt the coarse cloth of his bedsheets. The next moment was dark damask and velvet on his naked body, his back warmed by sun off the

Mediterranean blue. He turned her over and held her under him, laying her on curtain silk and a woven carpet, his hand under her head. Clothes were scattered over the marble, glowing in the late afternoon, her red dress and a man's clothes. But the man's clothes weren't the groundskeeper's work garments.

For a moment he worried that he was only her diversion, and that another man might be waiting for her just outside the frame of carmine-red curtains, ready to reclaim his garb. The clothes matched hers; the shirt was full-moon white, the trousers dark and the waistcoat the color of garnets. But before he could worry after the other man, she ran her hands over his shoulders and back. Cotton and damask appeared on him wherever she touched. She was dressing him with her fingers. The clothes appeared on his body like a bar of sun moving over the terrace. He returned her touch, and soon her rose garden of a dress covered her body. He'd barely caught his breath when she pulled him to his feet and down the steps, toward the wheat-colored beach.

The afternoon was clear and blue, like it had been swept clean by a storm. Drops of water beaded the sea oats. Their progress was slow; they barely made it along a stretch of sand before one of them stopped to find the other's lips. When they lay in the sand, her limbs moved softly as though she were swimming. Her own movement made her laugh. He smiled at the rare moments his touch or kiss surprised her enough to keep her still, slowly learning where he could touch her to make her bloom between her legs like a spray of lilacs.

It was a full day before anyone came looking for the young groundskeeper; the elder Mrs. Lawrence sent for him when her bed stand arrangement had wilted. They found only a seascape inside the frame that once held the painted woman, a seascape the younger Mrs. Lawrence liked well enough and thought adequately tasteful to hang in the foyer. She might have thought her husband had bought a new picture in apology. Or she might have been the only one who noticed the two small figures on a distant beach, a woman in a loosened dress who held a young man's hand as she led him along the amber shore. The painting caught them midstep, the moment before the woman pulled him into a cove of rockrose, out of view.

DOLLY

Charlotte Stein

I make him out of spit and straw and other things usually used
for fake magic, in movies. I make him out of bits of melted
wax and coal dust, and I do it for fun, for nothing—none of this
is real. Or at least, I'm sure it's not until I wake up in the middle
of the night and find my dolly sitting on the end of the bed.

I know it's him, because of the eyes. I made the eyes out of
tiny beads of amber, little things foraged from the bottom of
my mum's old jewelry box. And he has those exact same amber
eyes, almost liquid in the blue light from streetlamps.

Plus he seems to have a dusting of coal and straw all over
him—there's always that, for a clue. And when he opens his
mouth to speak, no sound comes out, as though his insides are
full up with melted wax and all of the other stupid things I
made him out of.

But other than that, he looks pretty real. He looks like a
man, a real man, with skin all honey colored—though I didn't
use honey, in my maybe-spell—and dark hair so soft, and thick,

and silky. He can't speak, but that's okay. I think I might have screamed, if he'd spoken in some kind of voice from beyond the grave, or voodoo scratch and growl. As it is I've stuffed myself up by the headboard and don't want to come down, in case he gets me.

This weird, magical dolly I didn't intend to make.

I say to him:

"Where have you come from?"

Which seems dumb, because I know where he came from. He came out of me and the thing I made, and the words I read from that little silly book on witchcraft—the one my mum left me, when she died. I was only intending to make a big wax doll that could do the hoovering for me, but I guess you never know what you're going to get until it's here.

You never know that reality's going to slide sideways, until it does.

"Make a sign, if you understand me," I say, even though I'm still not wholly convinced he's really there, on the end of my bed. He looks so solemn and silent, though, which makes it hard to imagine he's anything but actually in existence. His grave amber eyes follow my every movement, in a way that should probably be creepy, but isn't.

It isn't at all. Not even when he raises a hand and kind of... curls it, and somehow I know that means *I understand you.*

"Did you come out of the wax doll I made?" I blurt out, which seems even dumber than *where have you come from*, but there it is. I need to know. I need to hear it from his hands, even if I can see that the doll is no longer on my dresser. Of course it isn't. It's become him, instead.

"Did you—" I start to say, again, but he stops me midsentence. He curls his hand, and now it's certain that the gesture means *yes.*

Though I'm not sure why, it makes me slide back down into somewhere close to the middle of the bed, as if I'm no longer afraid. I am afraid, all right? I am. I'm not breathing hard, and my heart isn't racing in quite the same way, but I'm afraid, I'm sure.

"Are you, like, a golem?" I say, but this time he makes a different hand gesture. Like a stop sign, only with his palm turned to one side.

That means *no*. I'm sure it does. Something about him makes me sure, immediately, as though he's a part of me that I didn't know existed. A wish, I think, that I didn't know I wanted to make.

But it's made, now. It's too late. I've created my own personal Frankenstein's monster, only far prettier, and sweeter, and without a voice. And also a lot more naked, because when he stands up, suddenly, I can see *everything*.

He's not shy, my dolly. It's me who turns away, as though it's not all right to look.

He sleeps a lot, and usually in the day. It makes me think of vampires or some other awful supernatural creature I hadn't thought of, but he never does anything else to make me think he's going to suddenly eat me. I think, daily, that he's going to suddenly not exist, but that's different.

One is mildly disturbing. The other is terrifying. And I don't know which feeling applies to which event. I come home wondering if he's going to be gone and feel the stultifying nothingness of reality clawing at my throat, wringing through my bones, god. God.

Please don't take this one magical thing away from me. I don't care if I'm imagining it. Don't take it away.

I'm not sure how I so quickly came to this place, but it's

there, all the same. Maybe it has something to do with the way he gets things across to me, with quick hand gestures and this beautiful sort of miming. He'll let his eyes drift closed and his body sink down, to illustrate how tired he is, when I ask him why he needs to sleep so often. When I question him again on where he came from, he'll come up behind me and his hands will wave over my eyes, so that I can see the darkness coming.

And I understand, perfectly. He came from darkness. It's why the light bothers him, though he also tells me that it's bothering him less and less. *Soon,* he signs to me, *it will not bother me at all.*

So I say to him—*One day, will you be able to speak? Will other things change about you, until you're whole again?*

And he makes a gesture like a bird breaking from his chest—*hopefully*—just before he settles down in bed, beside me. I don't know when we started sleeping next to each other, but the apartment's only small and he's so big—I don't want him to be uncomfortable.

Of course I don't want him to be my giant sex doll, either, but that's something else altogether, isn't it? Sleeping with him curled around me like a big, warm comma isn't the same as taking advantage of a thing I made.

Though sometimes he stares at me through the darkness, with his liquid amber eyes, and I wonder what taking advantage really is. And who's doing it to whom.

It's on the twelfth night that I kiss him. I don't mean to. It's an accident. I turn over in bed and my mouth meets his, fumbling through the darkness. Almost as though he was just waiting there for me to turn over in a certain sort of way, with my head down and my mouth ready and *oops.*

I'm kissing something not-real. I'm kissing a doll. His lips feel just ever so slightly too cool for him to be truly human. But they're also soft, and there isn't even the slightest hint of wax or coal dust, and I can taste something like cinnamon even though he doesn't eat.

I want to ask him, immediately, where this taste came from, but he pulls away and puts a hand over my lips. He asks me to be silent, like him, so I obey. It seems only fair. And when he runs his hand down over my body and fondles my breasts through the thin material of my nightie, that seems fair, too.

Especially as I ache so much to touch him, so much that I actually do it without thinking. I touch his smooth, firm chest, and the almost-curve of his hip, and then his back, that great slab of a back. Sometimes when I see him from behind, bending over or reaching for something, I find myself mesmerized by the shape of his back. Such a tapering waist, and such broad shoulders!

And always without clothes, obviously. I'll be honest—I haven't even tried to get him to wear anything. If he's comfortable, why shouldn't he remain so? Why shouldn't I touch him back, if that makes him comfortable, too?

Because I'm fairly certain it does. I can hardly see him in the darkness—this time, the streetlamps are closed off by curtains—so I can't see his hands and what they're signing to me, but really we don't need signs. What do signs matter, when he's running his fingertips over the slight shape of my belly and down, farther down, all the way down?

Here is where I think a human man, a man who could speak would say—*Is this okay?* But of course he isn't, and he can't, and so here we are. I touch, and he touches. He touches, then I touch. It happens so quickly, I'm sure, and yet it feels as slow as moving through syrup.

His hands spread over me, and I can sense the curiosity in

them. It makes me feel as though *I'm* the doll, for a moment, *I'm* the one who came from the other side of nothing, and he's the one uncovering all of the things I'm made of.

I want to say to him, *sugar and spice and all things nice*, but I don't think that's true. I feel much more like snails and puppy dogs' tails, wicked as anything and eager for his fascinated touch. He plucks at the nightie until he's got it almost all the way off me, and I don't stop him. I let him explore my body, from the wet and aching slit between my legs, to all the hills and dips of my face.

He does it gently, slowly, and occasionally presses at places as though he's found something interesting—the tiny scar near my shoulder, from falling out of a tree when I was young; the dimples just above my bottom that seem as deep as canyons when I check them out in the mirror; the little black mark high up on my cheek, like a beauty spot, only not.

And once he's done mapping all of this with his fingers, and followed it with far more dirty and arousing things—a shivering stroke along the line of my lips, a caress through the folds of my sex—he tries it out with his mouth and his tongue. He kisses my mouth, then my cheeks, then the already arching turn of my throat. Then he moves down, to my breasts—and I can't help clasping at him, and pushing up at him.

I don't care what he's made of. This is...oh, it is.

He points his tongue and makes little circles around each of my nipples, until I'm biting back moans. I want to maintain the silence he's forced into, but it's crazily difficult when I can feel that his tongue isn't exactly the right texture. Unlike the rest of him—which feels perfectly, awesomely human—his tongue is just ever so slightly rough, and it burrs along my skin like something sweet and terrible, all at the same time.

He dips it into my belly button and runs it, wetly, along my sides, and it's all I can do to stop myself squirming. I don't want to squirm too much and put him off. I want to moan and show him it's good.

So I do. To hell with the silence. To hell with the idea that he's only licking me to get the taste, and then in a moment is going to devour me to please the ancient gods that allowed his creation. A million awful things could be true of him, and a million more delicious ones, but they all feel good, just the same. If he eats me in the end, at least I'll die in bliss.

And if he eats me in the other way, well. Who am I to complain? I won't argue with ancient gods. Instead I'll spread my legs and be more commanding with him than I've ever dared to be with any normal man. Maybe part of me feels awkward about using him in this way. But another part of me says go on, go on, because, well...he's not really my dolly, is he?

He's a part of me. He knows me. I can feel he does, in every hot breath he lets gust against my heated sex. He knows how to tease, and understands just how much I can take, and he doesn't even have to wait for me to squirm. I think he knows the squirm's coming before it does.

Then I put my hand in his hair and tug, just as I'm sure he knew I would. I need him close and touching me, and he knows that—he knows it enough to press one damp kiss to my bare sex, right at the curving apex of it all. It's close enough to my clit for me to feel something go through it, but not quite good enough.

Until he lets his tongue flicker out, and then it's good enough. That teasing, weird-rough tongue ghosts so close to my swollen little bead that I arch, and my hand tightens in his hair all of its own accord. I think I say something, then—something like *Please*, or an instruction, like *Lick me*—but he disobeys for just one terrible moment longer.

He isn't my dolly, really. He's his own thing—whatever that

is. And he licks when he wants to lick, pulls away when he wants to pull away, and when I moan, restlessly, that's when he finally gives in.

He slides his tongue the length of my sex, parting the lips there effortlessly, reaching my clit as though there's no such thing as tease. Instead there's pressing, and licking, and lapping, and when he flicks the underside with that burring velvet tongue, I do die. I disappear into bliss.

It's almost this side of pain, but that's okay. I think I like a little pain, and I like it more when he rakes his nails down the insides of my thighs and rubs his tongue against the tip of my clit in a way that almost burns. My body twists without my permission, and I reach out for my orgasm—the one that seems so achingly close—but of course he pulls it away at the last second. Of course he does.

I'm pretty sure I could predict every move he makes before it's made, but somehow I still feel surprised when he sits up and back. I feel for him through the darkness and find a hint of arm, a slide of his thigh. But it's his face that finally comes to my hands, his perfect lovely face. I know every line of it before I've touched it, and even though I can hardly see, I know the amber of his eyes. I know him, too, and I caress him with all of that knowledge in mind.

I don't tease, because he can't bear it the way I can. He's waited too long in nothingness, unlike me who's had it all, for so long. So I slide my fingers down his body and capture the thick stem of his cock in both hands, rubbing at the base and rubbing at the tip and making his breath gust hot against my upturned face.

It's a strange thing, to feel someone's reactions rather than hear them. It reminds me, oddly, of masturbation and having to keep quiet because someone's next door—the husband who bores you, your Great-Aunt Tilly staying over for Christmas, someone, anyone—and I think I like that. I like his sudden violent tremors and the way he shuffles on the bed, spreading his legs apart to give me more access.

I follow his lead and stroke that soft strip of skin behind his balls, and when his cock jerks up in my hand I rub harder. I rub until the tremors become shudders, and the head of his prick becomes slick to the touch.

It's just begging me to taste it. So I do. I bend down and feel for him blindly with my mouth, and when I finally taste him, my sex aches in sympathy. He's so stiff and tense against my tongue, so salty-sweet with precome, and he can't seem to help the little shove forward his body falls into.

But after, he seems to get a hold on himself. He moves away from me before I can stop him, and I feel the loss of his body in my mouth and all around me more keenly than I would have expected. I wave my arms around in the darkness, searching for him, but I know he's off the bed. I can hear his feet padding against the wooden floor, and he takes his time walking around the bed, before coming back to me.

By the time he leans in from somewhere to my right, I'm gasping for him and definitely breaking the silence. I get a hold of his arms and pull him down on top of me, and he doesn't resist. His mouth finds mine and his hands slide over my back, and I'm sure I briefly feel that deliciously hard cock slide between my legs. Something thick passes over the slick mess of my sex, and then our bodies are pressed tight together on the bed—too tight to breathe.

I feel as though we're merging together—and maybe we are, who knows?—shortly before he bumps his hips and his prick finds the groove of my sex more solidly, then slides down to that waiting hollow...oh.

I have the briefest feeling that we shouldn't be doing this, though I don't know why. He feels good and right inside me, and it both exacerbates and soothes the ache still thrilling through me. There's nothing wrong with this, I'm sure there isn't, and when he moves I'm made doubly so.

He goes at it with all the passion he can't speak of, one hand shakily gripping my hip, the other above my head somewhere. His hips churn and his breath wavers over my upturned face, strongly cinnamon and almost like a furnace, by this point.

But that's okay, because my body feels like one, too. I'm burning from the inside out and feel sure that if I were made of wax, as he was, I'd have long since melted away. And then his hand slinks between our bodies, and I feel something brush over my clit—just once, but once is enough. It's more than enough.

I call out the name he doesn't have. My body shakes with it, the way his is doing, and it takes only a minute more of his erratic thrusts for him to give in, too. His body goes tense and tight all over, and his cock swells inside me, all of which feels good. It feels better than good. Even without the thing he does next, I'm wrung out and suffused with the warmest, oddest sort of pleasure I've ever felt.

But it definitely intensifies when a word stumbles brokenly from somewhere deep inside him.

"Sophie," he says, and it's the strangest thing. It feels like the first time I've ever heard someone calling my name, even though I hear it every day. It feels like I'm brand new again, and that's okay.

I'll be brand new, with him. I'll be me, with him.

He tells me his name is Dune, but I don't think he's saying it right. I don't think I'm hearing it right. His words come slow and as broken as that first time, and he has no explanations for me.

Of course he doesn't. I don't know why I expected otherwise.

I don't know why I care. Though in truth, I don't. I don't care about anything but his hands on me, and his mouth on me, and even though reality is melting away in the face of all of those things, I don't care about that, either.

But the worst thing is...the worst thing is, I don't care even though I know he's hiding something. In fact, I catch him doing it. One day I come home early—I'm going to lose my job, soon, because I can never wait until the proper clock-out time to leave, now—and he's been in the bedroom, but he pretends he hasn't. He comes out blustering and trying to say a whole bunch of words that don't suit him:

Didn't. What. You're home early.

Those sorts of words.

So naturally I wait until he's asleep in front of some colorfully flickering television program, looking as peaceful as can be and as perfect as always. Then I go into the bedroom neither of us has been in since I came home and caught him, and just look around. I don't know what it is I'm expecting to find, but I get the weirdest feeling. Like when I was a kid, and maybe I was doing something with my dollies that I shouldn't have been—cutting their hair or making them kiss.

That's what I see behind my eyes, when I think of him emerging from the bedroom, guilt-stricken.

And then I see one of the floorboards, just ever so slightly askew; just a little bit—nothing much, really.

Enough to make me frightened, I'll admit. I pretend I don't know, but I do, really. I can hear it like a hidden heart, beating. I'm in an Edgar Allan Poe story, and I just didn't know it.

Though I know what I expect to find under the floorboards. It's going to be the doll, isn't it? It's going to be the doll I made—he didn't come from it after all. It's all just a lie; he's some con man or weirdo or something, something awful.

And so I don't know what to make of what I do find, under there. I can't tell if it's awful or not—I don't even know what it signifies, at first. I mean, I find the doll I made of him—of course I do. I'm pretty sure he put it under here, for god knows what purpose. But I'm stopped from thinking he's a con man or trying to be sly or something like it, by what I find next to his doll.

Of course I recognize it immediately—it's not as though I don't understand what it is. It's a dolly, another dolly, laid next to his wax effigy as though it was always meant to be there. As though it loves his doll as much as I love him, passionately, madly, insanely.

Only it's dusty, as though it's been there forever, and it's far slighter than the one I made. It's wearing a pretty flowery dress, like the one I had as a child, and it has dark eyes like specks of jet. Dark hair, too, and on its cheek—or the place where its cheek should be—is a little black mark.

Like a beauty spot, only not.

LA BELLE MORT

Zander Vyne

Young woman, you do realize, if you could be with child, you may plead your belly?" The judge had tired eyes.

Eliza remained quiet, and the audience tittered.

"Very well. Lady Elizabeth Jane Morton, you are sentenced to be taken hence to the prison in which you were last confined where, after three Sundays have passed, you will be hanged by the neck until dead. May the Lord God have mercy upon your soul."

Gypsy...succubus...witch—murmurs, as she was led away.

Had they looked beyond the snow-white skin, wild black curls, and eerie calm, they would have seen the bones of her knuckles shining through her skin; she held her hands clenched painfully tight to keep from lashing out at all of them and going absolutely mad.

A cell to myself at the end of a narrow, gloomy hall. Dank, always cold. Oozing drips stain the walls rust-brown. Insanity— cackles, moans and screams. Fleas, mice and slithering sounds in the darkness. A cot and rough blanket. A long bench to sit upon. Small comforts from Charity Ladies, mercifully none familiar to me. They bring gifts, the smell of perfume, and pity. I accept them all. Today's treasures—ink, quill pens and paper. Solace found.

Eliza fought slumber; it crawled with dark dreams and beckoned with greedy fingers. Hours, long and black, were spent struggling to cling to awareness, her life dwindling away.

Regrets stung. Time was short, and peace was as elusive as life. Insanity promised everlasting oblivion, and she was tempted to succumb as so many had around her. Writing gave her temporary respite. There was no one to write, so she wrote for herself; poems, thoughts, lists and letters she would never send.

> *Dear Lord Dover,*
>   *Do you sleep peacefully? Do your children fare well without their nursemaid in their nursery? Despite what you have done, my prayers are with their poor little souls.*
>   *I wonder where you hid the necklace and if it calls to you in your dreams. Will it haunt you, as surely I will if there is a God and he grants wishes?*
>   *My life is forfeit, and still I would rather this death than your wrinkled hands upon me.*
>
> *Lady Elizabeth Jane Morton*

She folded scribbled-upon paper into tiny paper birds, and sailed them into the courtyard. Sometimes, they landed in the shadows of the gallows themselves, but usually the wind caught them and carried them away to join the plentiful refuse littering London's streets.

GOOD THINGS
Father
Mayfair House
London
Carriages
Ball gowns
The Waltz
Flirting
James
The Dover children

BAD THINGS
This place

A "new" dress—bodice too tight, tattered skirt. A string to tie my hair off my neck—blessed relief. Small things mean so much now.

She documented everything, writing furiously, clinging to sanity.

A hanging—crowd swelling, sudden and boisterous, fathers lifting children upon their shoulders, vendors selling meat-pies and posies. It was like a country fair, everyone smiling, fun in the air.

Her mind screamed, "Don't! Look away!" but she was compelled to watch.

They led the prisoner out. His head was down, but Eliza saw the glistening tears on his death-pale flesh. Placed under the gallows, his feet centered atop the wooden trapdoor, he wept openly.

His legs were pinioned, to prevent his soon-to-be flailing feet from finding purchase on the brick-lined walls of the famous Long Drop below. The noose was fitted; a large knot of rope adjusted to rest, just so, beneath his left ear.

The hangman—cloaked in black—the very specter of death. The prisoner wailed—a high-pitched whine—when the hood was placed over his head. Did he open his eyes then, when the cloth covered his face? Did his lashes catch on the fabric, and did he take it in his mouth, dry and musky, as he gulped air, grunting and snorting? Did each prisoner have a new hood, or did that frantic man, about to die, smell the deaths that had come before his, lingering in the cloth?

Ghastly, snapping sound ringing out of the pit. Imagined? Surely so; the crowd had cheered when the man fell out of sight.

Life passes too slowly, too quickly. What prayer will save me from this fate?

Eliza was sleeping the first time he came, at dusk.

"Do not be afraid."

She was—trapped in here, weak from lack of real food and sunshine; she was helpless.

The man sat on the narrow bench. He was rather fine looking, his face somewhat stern and his clothing somber. A cleric, Eliza decided, calming.

"Has that much time passed? It must have, for them to send you."

"I want to help you."

She held back a bitter reply; no one could help her. "I do not believe in God."

"I am the only one you need believe in." He spread his hands wide, as if to dare her to argue that he was anything less than flesh and blood.

Eliza remained silent, and he reached into his pocket, pulling out a square of paper. He read, "Life passes too slowly, too quickly. What prayer will save me from this fate?"

"That is mine!" Eliza bolted from the cot.

Too slow. He tucked the note into the folds of his coat. "Yes, I know."

He handed her another scrap of paper, his fingertips brushing her wrist as it changed hands.

Her cheeks flooded with color, and she escaped his gaze, reading the words on the page.

> *Proud beauty, angel amidst foul circumstance.*
> *I hear you calling,*
> *and know you weep.*
> *Let me guide you in your dark journey,*
> *and give you peace in this dread.*
> *In your ruin, find faith in me.*

What manner of cleric was this?

"I told you, I do not have faith."

"And I told you, have faith in *me*."

"I do not understand."

He lifted his hand, tracing the path a tear made down her cheek.

Eliza held very still, quivering under his fingertips.

"You do not have to understand, Lizalamb."

She blinked. He'd called her Lizalamb, just like her father had a lifetime ago. How odd.

"I'm afraid."

"Of course you are, but you can conquer your fears and all will be well. This I promise. Have *faith*."

He freed the string she had used to tie her hair back, and reached into his pocket once more.

Red ribbons, bows that give girlish pleasure. His voice gruff as he gifted them. What a strange, fascinating man.

Eliza nibbled on her bottom lip, the treasures clutched in her hand, red ends trailing from her fist. "Will they let me keep them?"

"Yes, Liza. No one will bother you anymore."

"Thank you."

A pail of warm water, beside it—wrapped with care—a whole bar of jasmine scented soap.

Eliza plaited the scarlet ribbons into her hair. She waited, writing.

> *A stranger, in my darkest hour,*
> *offering peace for my faith,*
> *scarlet ribbons to tie my hair.*
> *My fate is unchangeable, measured in rope and wood,*
> *the dozen yards to my doom.*
> *Rise above, fall below.*
> *The silent clock keeps ticking.*
> *Yet, something about him—sanctuary;*
> *already, I am anxious for his return,*
> *to feel as I did in those brief moments,*
> *when his hands held mine.*
> *Hopeful.*

Finally, he came.

It was night. She was sleeping.

"Close your eyes." He placed his hand over them.

Eliza struggled, pushing him away.

He let her go, holding up his lantern.

More handsome than remembered. A trick of light or a young

girl's heart finding something of desire's fancy in these last days?
Lust, peace, comfort. His voice—an anchor in the night.

"You can control your reaction to fear if you control your
mind. You need not face the unknown at all if you have a place
within yourself of peace and serenity, and a means to find it.
Change what you *think*, and you change what you feel." He
opened the little door in the lantern and blew out the flame
within. "Close your eyes."

This time she obeyed.

Days, hours and precious little life left. What is the harm in
doing as he asks?

His fingers skimmed her hair. She whimpered, but did not
move away.

"Think of a place, familiar, happy and safe. Go there in your
mind. Picture it, smell it, feel it."

Mayfair House—Father, servants, old wood and lemon oil,
laughter, parties and endless possibilities. Death, ruin, empty,
sold, gone.

"I have no safe places."

She had struggled in this place to find tranquility as memories crashed in on her, and she wanted more than anything to
think of something else. Anything else.

"Then make believe. Tell me where you would be, if you
could be anywhere you desired."

His smell—crisply clean, manly under soap. A sudden
image—him, standing in a lake, surrounded by a meadow
dotted with tansies, forget-me-nots and lemon balm. The sky
above is endless, blue. His hair is loose, dark. He is naked.

"Ahhh," she sighed.

"Tell me."

"No!"

"Why not?"

"Because!"

"This I definitely wish to hear. Tell me." His voice held a new teasing note that sent prickles down her arms.

"Well," she said, clearing her throat. "I saw a meadow of wildflowers and a lake, bluer than the sky."

"And?"

"You were there."

"Me? What was I doing?"

"You were in the lake."

"Drowning?"

He was not old, but he was not young either. A cleric, surely he had heard lustful thoughts before.

"No, bathing I think."

"Naked?"

"Of course! Clothing would be silly indeed if one were bathing."

"What were you doing, besides watching me?"

"That was all I was doing!"

"No picnic, no flower gathering or cloud watching?"

"Oh, yes! We supped on steak and kidney pies, Devonshire cheeses, and exotic fruit sent in from India." She laughed.

"What eclectic tastes you have! Did I kiss you?"

"Oh, my...yes. We kissed and kissed," she said, her voice dreamy and girlish to her ears.

"And, were you joyful then, Lizalove?"

"Yes. Yes, I was," she answered, faintly surprised.

The next time he came, he carried a rope.

"Is this one of the things you fear?"

"Yes." Her gaze darted to the coil of twine.

He placed it on her lap, the ends snaking to the ground. Her fingers shrunk away.

"Tell me what you fear."

"The way it will feel. The weight of it, the roughness of it, the finality of it."

"Do you trust me?"

What is it about him? I am girlish and hopeful, excited to greet the day, because he might fill it. Be he cleric or devil, man or beast, in these last days he gives things believed lost forever. I am drowning, willingly.

"Yes."

He took the rope from her, his fingers lingering over hers. Her flesh tingled, from his hand to her belly, and between her legs.

He made a loop of the rope and hung it around her neck.

She did not move.

He bunched up her skirt with one hand and held the rope with the other. She met his gaze and spread her legs wider. She wanted his touch, no matter what that made her, or him.

His hand slid up the rope until his knuckles brushed the skin under her chin. His other hand curled around her inner thigh, fingers walking a silken path. He pinched her and petted her, and she did not move.

"In fear can be found pleasure, just as in darkness can be found light."

Eliza felt the truth of his words as the rope around her neck tightened, the hemp scratchy. Like whiskers, they licked her. She no longer cared about the rope because of what his other fingers did. Her head lolled back against the wall.

"Do you feel it?" His breath kissed her cheek.

Eliza jutted her hips to his hand.

"Yesss." She watched him lick his lips as he slid his fingers into the hot clutch of her body.

"Yes, Lizalove. You feel it." His eyes were obsidian darkness.

Torture—spread wide for him, still, not flinging myself upon him. He gave what was needed yet held back. I know there is more. Twin sighs as fingers pushed inward, curling within. He did not ask about the lack of barrier.

"Is the rope a concern now?"

"Nooo..."

Languid, craving the pleasure—forbidden delights. His lips curving against mine, tongue slipping between. Suckling him, an arm looped around his neck, fingers winding in the tangle of his dark hair.

"You can find this place too, anytime you wish. Squeeze your cunnie around my fingers."

Cunnie—a startling word, naughty. I like it and think, had I the time, I might find that I am a very, very bad girl after all.

Her flesh gripped his fingers, and new pleasures bloomed. His thumb nudged high in her cleft, burning.

"Oh, god...please."

"Yes indeed, Eliza. Soon, soon." He withdrew his fingers.

She started to pull her thighs together, but he stopped her, tightening the rope around her throat.

"Not yet."

She shuddered and stayed spread wide.

"Do you touch yourself in the night, Lizalove? Right there?" His hand cupped her yearning flesh again.

"Yesss."

"What do you think of?"

"Youuu..." She could not lie to him.

He removed the loop of rope from her neck.

"Think of the darkness, think of the rope, think of my cock," he said.

"Ohhh."

When she opened her eyes, he was gone.

She went straight to bed.

* * *

Losing track of time, sun and moon changing places. He has not returned. Found out? Had all he wanted? Maybe something has happened to him. I do not even know his name.
    Wondrous gift. A note from him:

> *How can this be?*
> *I mourn what is not yet gone!*
> *Emptied by the future that does not hold you.*
> *Do I risk hell for a heaven here and now?*
> *Dare I tempt the rope?*
> *I find you guilty of only one thing, angelic thief;*
> *you have taken my heart and wherever you are,*
> *I know, there shall my heart be too.*
> *Fear not the darkness—I am the dark,*
> *and you are my secret, eternal.*
> *I will set you free.*
> *Give all to me.*

Still, the Cleric does not come.

A new visitor. Why am I so afraid when they tell me?

No formal visiting rooms here; Charity Ladies, physicians, clerics and visitors all came to the condemned's cell when audience was desired.

    Nothing to tidy, no mirror to check, knowing she had never been dirtier or more ashamed, she stood with her cheek pressed to the bars so she could see who the guard led to her.

    James Thomas, Lord Dover's gardener and her erstwhile suitor.

    Her knees went weak. She crumpled to the dusty floor; the

only thing keeping her from falling was her grip on the metal doors.

Shouldn't she at least be allowed a choice? She was to die. Should she not be given the right to refuse a visitor? She only wished to see the Cleric.

She closed her eyes and, only because she refused to be found by anyone groveling in the dirt, she lifted herself up and was standing when the doors opened.

"James." She wished she had it in her to tell him to leave. Leave now and never come back, never think of her again like this. It would be easier for them both.

James

Sweet, sweet boy.

"Eliza, I came as soon as they would allow it!"

He did not offer his hand or a hug, and that was not surprising. His courtship had been most proper. It was not in his nature to be overly demonstrative.

James Thomas had an innocence about him that still tugged at Eliza's heartstrings, though she was not in love with him. On the Dover estates, their paths had crossed often. She spent much of her time out of doors with the children, and James was always to be found rallying the score of servants who attended to Lord Dover's expansive gardens wherever the family was in residence.

She had gently rebuffed his overtures, her heart still wounded over her father's death and the sudden changes in her life without him, though a part of her had started to warm. James was so sweet, good and kindly. He would make someone a very fine husband, she had started to think.

"You should not have come." She started to say more, but realized that was all there really was to say. Anything they might have had was best forgotten. He should go. She turned away from him.

"I had to come! They have not found Lady Dover's necklace. Lord Dover says if you wish to return home, you know what to do. I guess he means tell them where you hid it, but you cannot have done what they say. Not you. You're a good person, Eliza, I just know it." His brown eyes softened, though worry bracketed them with a thicket of frown lines.

Lord Dover had sent him. Sent James to tell her to acquiesce to his demands. For that was what his coded message meant. *Sleep with me. Be my Mistress and all will be forgotten. You can come home again.*

Could he really do that, she wondered. Have the Court reverse her sentence? Yes. She supposed a man as powerful as Lord Dover, who had managed to get her convicted of theft without any evidence, could do that.

All she would have to do was sleep with him. Not just once, for that she may have been able to stomach, but many times, for as long as he desired her. She would have to let the old man do anything he wished with her, anything at all, or it would be back to prison.

When her father died, and Lord Dover had offered her the post as nursemaid to his brood, he had seemed so kindly, her father's old friend, sympathetic to her loss and change of status. With nowhere else to turn, she had gratefully accepted the position.

Very soon, it became apparent that the old man had motives other than kindliness. His pursuit of her had been relentless. After he tried to sneak into her chambers one night, despite having nowhere to go, Eliza had been on the verge of fleeing when he had sprung the theft trap, and had her arrested.

He had made her the same offer before the authorities had arrived to take her away. *Sleep with me. Be my Mistress, and all will be forgotten.*

"James, you may tell Lord Dover I did not take the necklace." She would still rather die than be his plaything. Maybe she had gone insane after all in this place.

"Eliza! There must be a way to stop this nonsense. You cannot hang for something you did not do!" Emotion seemed to overcome him, and he reached for her hand, which she allowed him to hold for a moment before gently pulling away.

"Please, just go."

"I wanted us to marry, you know," his voice broke when he spoke.

"James, you barely know me. You need to forget about me."

"How can I? I love you." He made to reach for her again, and she moved away, unable to face the pain in his gentle brown eyes.

Once she had dreamed of love, and marriage. Back then, she would have rebuffed this boy's advances, preferring to dally with the affections of older, richer men. The daughter of a Lord, she had her pick of powerful, handsome suitors, and had been sure she had plenty of time to settle on the right match.

"James, I do not love you. You are a gardener. Nothing changes that. You and I were never meant to be together. Had my circumstance been different, I would not have deigned to even speak with you." Harsh words, meant to hurt, and not entirely true, for she had always been nice to everyone. They were words designed to send him away, to make him think of her no more.

"How can you say that? You were always so kind. So nice. I could tell you liked me too." His look of bemused hurt almost made her stop.

"Like I told you before, you never really knew me at all. Now, go. Please. Deliver my message to Lord Dover and forget all about me."

"Eliza!"

"Guard! He's ready to leave." She did not watch as he was taken away and would not have seen even had she looked. Tears flooded her vision and choked her breathing.

Though she had not loved James, in him she had glimpsed the possibility of a future, of a life without her father that, while different, would be livable. Sending him away, she finally allowed herself to mourn all of her losses. Her tears did not stop for days. More than once, she was tempted to give in to Lord Dover's demands so that she might live.

And still, the Cleric did not return.

I would give him anything. My dreams are filled with images of him, naked in the darkness. He is all I have left. He is all I desire.

A pail of warm water, beside it—wrapped with care—a whole bar of jasmine scented soap.

He's coming.

When she woke the moon was high, and he was there. He stood near the window. Beyond him, she saw falling snowflakes.

She moved to one side of the cot, telling him in the action exactly what she wanted from him.

He was upon her before she could let out a breath. He pulled up her skirt and they crashed together. Their mouths clung, and their hands clutched. His whiskers abraded her skin. She arched into the pain of it, needing him with a violence that was frightening.

He ran his hands slowly over her body. Eliza thought he meant to be tender then, and she did not want his kindness. She wrapped her fingers around his arms, her torn nails ripping into his flesh, dragging him down to her.

He fisted his hands in her hair and yanked her into place

beneath him. She spread her legs wide, welcoming him like the whore she had been called.

He devoured her mouth, leaving it only to lick his way to her nipples, biting and suckling them through the bodice of her dress, until she moaned, forcing him to clasp his hand over her mouth. He undid his trousers. She felt the heat of him slide into her. There was no pain, only a sense of fullness and pleasure.

He rose over her, propping himself up upon his hands. She opened her mouth to lick a corded muscle in his arm. A droplet of sweat seeped from his skin, and she savored its salt on her tongue.

She came, in a flood—sudden, harsh and sweet—and then so did he, lifting himself out of her, stroking his cock as he knelt between her thighs, shooting his seed onto her belly.

"Lizalove." He kissed the bruises his passion had left upon her.

"I do not even know your name." She rubbed his release into her flesh.

"William."

"Thank you, William."

Another day.

"There is one more thing, Liza."

She nodded.

I will give him anything he wishes for, and not ask a single question. I will do anything he wants; this is all I will ever have.

He wrapped his fingers around her throat, his other hand delving between her thighs.

"Hold your breath, Lizalove. Do not breathe for as long as you can, until you grow dizzy."

William kissed her, pushing his breath into her mouth, showing her how to breathe, slowly and deeply. She took his breath into her body, holding it when he squeezed her throat. It was difficult, not gasping for air, not panting with lust, but she looked into his eyes, and found euphoria in the control he showed her. She went with him to the place he had shown her, the peaceful meadow. His fingers worked magic, and her body opened for his bunched, fucking fingers.

Before it was over, he pushed his cock into her, choking her as he took her. He came flooding into her body just as she was overtaken by darkness.

"Breathe," he said, giving her his own breath until hers returned to normal.

He held her. "I wish I could do more," he said, as she closed her eyes to shut out everything but him. "Just remember, there is always light, after the darkness. *Always*."

And, for the first time, Eliza believed.

They came for her later, the hangman's assistant and the warden.

They tied her hands behind her back, and led her into the morning sun. Her feet made clumsy imprints in the blanket of blinding white snow. The air was crisp and cold. Eliza saw her breath—a warm fog of life she walked through before she closed her eyes.

The crowd cheered but she was far away, at a pristine lake, with a man who loved her. Flowers bloomed all around them, and she wore red ribbons in her hair.

Under the gallows, she breathed deeply, calmly, until peace flooded her. She opened her eyes again when the hangman placed his hand upon her shoulder.

Eliza looked into his eyes—death's eyes, the hangman's eyes, William's eyes.

"Have *faith*," she heard him whisper.

Then there was only darkness.

THE
PERSISTENCE
OF MEMORY

Evan Mora

The first time I saw her, she was lying on her back in a dirty
London alleyway, knife pressed against her throat, skirt
bunched to her waist. Her legs moved weakly, flashes of pale
skin visible through the torn fabric of her tights. A trickle of
blood welled at the knifepoint and traced a slow path down her
neck.

"Please..." she said, so softly it was all but a whisper, but I
heard it as clearly as if she'd breathed it into my ear; felt that
single syllable tingle all the way down my spine. Crude laughter
met her plea, the rasp of a zipper an ominous promise of the
horrors in store.

I've never abided that kind of violence, so I tore out her
assailant's throat, feasting on him with a ruthlessness befitting
his actions. He died quickly, his hand still wrapped around his
cock, eyes wide and unseeing, a wet, gurgling hiss bubbling out
of the wreckage of his neck as I tossed his limp body aside and
the last bit of air left his lungs.

I dreaded the next part. I waited for her to scream, perceiving me to be an evil greater than the monster who'd come so close to defiling her only moments ago. It had happened before. The evil that men do could at least be comprehended, whereas I...I was the stuff of nightmares.

But she didn't scream.

"Thank you," she said. My eyes shot to hers and I found myself falling into gentle, dove-gray depths. It was a sensation not unlike stepping off the ledge of a tall building. She was mesmerizing. I turned away, wiping a self-conscious hand across my face, cleaning it of blood as best I could before turning to look at her once more.

Her left eye was already beginning to swell, and would undoubtedly be a vivid purple-black by morning; her lower lip was split and there was an angry looking gash across her cheekbone. Yet despite all this her beauty shone like a beacon through the darkness, and I knew, as surely as the moon holds sway over the tides, that this waif of a girl could hold equal power over me.

After learning where she lived, I carried her to her home cradled against my chest, and she murmured her assent when I asked if I could come in.

"Will you tell me your name?" she asked.

"I am called Rowan," I told her.

"I'm Lily," she said.

Her room was small, scarcely furnished but for a bed beneath the window and an easel against the opposite wall, paints and canvasses in various states of completion taking up the rest of the space in the tiny student flat.

She flinched neither when I lay her in the center of her bed, nor when I cupped her cheek and stroked a gentle thumb across her torn skin.

"I can heal this, if you let me," I said, lost again in the soft innocence of her eyes. She nodded without speaking, and brushed her fingers across my lips, unleashing a trembling within me that I'd not felt in a century. I leaned in closer, the scent of her intoxicating, and whispered for her not to be frightened.

"I will never fear you," she whispered in my ear. "You are an angel come to save me."

I kissed her wound, laved it with my tongue, drew the taste of her into me with a shudder. And when that was healed and I raised myself up, she ran her tongue over the split in her lip.

"And this?" she asked. "Can you heal this too?" Desire was a sweet ache that coiled in my belly.

At the touch of my tongue to the abrasion on her lip, her mouth opened shyly beneath me, a temptation I could not have resisted even if I'd tried. I kissed her tenderly, stroking my tongue softly against hers and into the deeper recesses of her mouth, the faint trace of her blood still therein. Despite the generous feeding I'd had in the alley, hunger crawled beneath my skin, and my canines lengthened of their own accord.

"No!" I broke the kiss and reared back, unwilling to be the cause of any additional hurt she suffered this night.

"What is it?" She sat upright, scanning the room for signs of trouble and, finding none, settled her quizzical gaze on me.

"I should leave…" Certainly I should have. Instead I found myself reaching out, touching her hair, which fell to her shoulders in waves the color of sunlight. Every time I looked at her, she seemed more and more beautiful.

"I don't want you to go."

I closed my eyes against a wave of longing so intense it was all I could do not to press her back onto the bed and cover her body with mine, loving her with my mouth and hands until dawn spilled over the eastern horizon.

I might still have had a chance, even then; I believe that. But then she crawled into my lap and wrapped her arms around my neck.

"Please..." she said. And I was lost.

Hours later, when dawn was indeed threatening and I had extricated myself from her warm, slumberous embrace, I paused to look at her one last time. Her body bore no signs of the night's events, neither the horrible violence of the alley, nor the more tender violence of our coupling, I had made sure of that. Her lips were swollen, and she would no doubt be sensitive in places, but nothing that would give her overmuch pause.

I bent over her, feathering my thumb over the pulse point in her throat, my body clenching with remembered ecstasy at the memory of my teeth penetrating the flesh there.

"Lily... " I called her name in a melodious voice, speaking to her subconscious without waking her. "When you awake it will be without memory of last night, or..." I stumbled unexpectedly, "or me." How I wished it could be different!

"Your evening was uneventful, and you retired early with a headache. That is all." Her brow furrowed momentarily and she shifted restlessly in her sleep, as though resisting the suggestion; as though she were struggling to hold on to the memories that were vanishing from her mind like so many wisps of smoke. Then she was peaceful once more, and I took my leave, knowing that while she would not remember this night, I would almost certainly never forget.

I watched her. In the beginning, I told myself it was so I could be sure she was all right, thin justification to be sure, but altruistic enough to let my conscience rest easy. Autumn turned to winter, and winter to spring, and justification fell away forgotten as the waif from the alley, the girl in whose arms I'd known such peace, became an obsession. Lily was fleshed out, her substance and detail intimately ingrained in me. Her warmth and compassion; the focus and concentration she applied to her studies and painting alike; the grace with which she carried herself; the elegant line of her profile; the husky sound of her laughter: I knew it all. To look upon her filled me with more warmth than the heat of any fire, and the memory of her taste sustained me more than any blood I took through all the long winter nights.

What would it be like, I wondered, to let her know me? To have her walk beside me? It had been so long since I'd had a companion that I could scarcely remember what it was to share a life, a bed, even simple conversation. Such happiness seldom gifted my kind.

In the beginning...in the beginning we are all enamored of our strength and vitality and the prospect of eternity. It's human nature to want to share that with someone; it was how I'd been made, and I in turn had been no exception, passing on my blood to my lover filled with romantic ideals of forever. But we are not human, though conscience and human sensibility remains, and in the end, very few of us have the strength to endure the passage of centuries and the endless horror of the blood. I'd lost my maker and lover both. They'd gone willingly into the sun, weeping bloodstained tears and whispering a quiet *no more*.

I wouldn't condemn Lily to that fate, no matter how much I wanted her, no matter how lonely I was. She deserved to live a life filled with warmth and light, waking each morning wrapped in a loving embrace, raising fat babies and growing old on a front-porch swing. But though I wouldn't bring her into my world, I found I couldn't entirely leave hers either.

And so I watched her, this girl, from the dark, from the shadows. Seasons became years, and I watched her finish college, watched her working late into the night at the coffee shop across the street from her flat to supplement her income as a young artist. I watched, in time, as she fell in love with another woman, watched their passion burn brightly and then fade, watched the arguments, and finally, watched the end.

I watched her cry, my Lily, and felt my heart breaking right along with hers. Her pain, perhaps even more than her happiness, drew me to her, just as it had that night in the alley. And she was hurting so much... how could I do other than help ease her sorrows?

She sat alone at a table in a corner of the deserted coffee shop, midnight long past, her face buried in her hands, quiet sobs wracking her small frame. I waited at the counter until she noticed me and hastily wiped her tears away, offering me a sad smile and a halfhearted shrug of her shoulders as she took her place opposite me at the counter.

"One of those days, you know?" she offered by way of explanation.

"Only too well," I replied.

Her eyes had not rested on me directly in nearly three years, and yet I felt their impact as immediately and fully as I had before; felt myself falling into their silvery depths.

"Are you okay?" she asked, a slight wariness edging her tone.

"I should be asking you that." I smiled compassionately, animating my features and shifting my weight from one foot to the other. There is an unnatural stillness that we acquire over time—I didn't know how long I'd been looking at her, long enough at least to make her nervous.

"I'll be all right." She'd eased visibly when I moved. "I just have a little way to go yet."

I sat with her. Listened to her. Fell in love with her all over again. At length, the shop closed and we walked aimlessly through the night, and she seemed as loath as I to end our time together, though perhaps she just didn't want to be alone. Eventually we arrived at her flat, and there was a charged silence between us. I could have filled it with more conversation, platitudes, any number of things. Instead, I did the thing I had ached to do all night. I kissed her.

I telegraphed my intentions, moving slowly and purposefully toward where she stood with her back against the door, cupping her face between my hands and giving her ample opportunity to protest. Her breath hitched slightly and she laid her hands on my abdomen, but she didn't push me away.

"Please—" she whispered, naked need in her voice, and I covered her mouth with mine, stealing her breath and any other words she might have spoken.

No tenderness, no gentle explorations. We kissed with a desperation born of pain and loneliness, a fiery gnashing of teeth and tongues. Her hands fisted into my shirtfront and she moaned into my mouth, sending tendrils of fire racing along my skin. I pressed into her, the space between our bodies too much to bear, and moaned at the sweet crush of her breasts against mine. She shifted slightly so that my thigh was between hers and she ground herself against me, her hot fingers tunneling beneath my shirt, burning a path across my sides, nails digging crescent moons deep in my back.

I broke the kiss with a hiss, reveling in the tiny hurt, nipping her lower lip in turn, watching hungrily as blood welled and her tongue swept out to collect it, carrying it back into the dark warmth of her mouth. A growl rose out of the depths of my chest and I slanted my mouth across hers once more, my tongue delving deeply, chasing her sanguine heat, unable to suppress a moan as the heady taste of her, so unlike any other, flooded my senses.

Need was a living thing clawing at my insides. I had to get

closer. I needed her skin. My tongue traced the line of her jaw; my canines scraped the soft skin at her throat and a trembling began in my core, the seductive pounding of her pulse beneath my lips an irresistible siren call. My arms tightened convulsively around her waist and she gasped, grinding against me all the harder, pulling at my clothing, incoherent pleadings hot against my ear.

Great as the need was to feel her blood run against my tongue, it paled in comparison to the need to feel her body stretched out against mine; to let the heat from her skin seep into me and ease the cold ache that had lived inside me since I'd left the warmth of her bed these three years ago. There was only her. There would only ever be her.

"Lily..." Her name was a whispered litany on my lips, a breath of sound pressed against the naked curve of her breast, into the secret hollow of her hip, and against the burning center of her.

"More," she cried softly, body undulating beneath me on the bed, the blush of arousal coloring her pale skin, blonde hair a tangled halo on the pillow.

Cradled between her thighs, I drank her in, revisiting the landscape of her femininity with my tongue, my own sex pulsing with need as I traced the length of her with long strokes, then delved deeper, pushing into her core until I could go no farther, and her hands held my head tightly to her while she came apart around me with a low, keening cry.

"More..." she cried again, and I replaced tongue with fingers, thrusting into her and scraping my teeth against the engorged tissue of her clitoris. I drew her into my mouth and settled into a rhythm of firm steady strokes, feeling tension draw her body tight like a bow once more, and the answering tension coiling hot and hard in me.

"It's not enough..." Her head thrashed slowly from side to side on the pillow, and her hands fisted into the bedsheets, helpless tears pooling and falling from the corners of her eyes.

"Sshhh..." I whispered, kissing my way from the soft skin of her inner thigh upward and across her taut belly, lavishing attention on each of her high firm breasts, taking first one, then the other dusky pink nipple into my mouth, suckling each tight peak until the desire to pierce her flesh and taste her blood was all but overwhelming.

"Closer..." she pleaded, "I need you closer..." Her hands were in my hair, pulling me up so that we were kissing once more, our bodies fused from breast to hip, our legs intertwined, my fingers sliding deep into her waiting heat.

It was my turn to cry out as Lily's hips rose to meet my thrusts and her thigh pressed tight between my legs, crushing my clitoris against her and slicking her flesh with the sheen of my arousal. My hips rocked forward helplessly, and I felt the twin tails of bloodlust and orgasm lash together at the base of my spine and become inextricably entwined.

"Lily!" I cried, thrusting into and against her with deep, powerful strokes, knowing I wouldn't be able to stop, her pleas for more a desperate chant in my ear.

"I'm so sorry..." I said against her throat, scraping her heated flesh with my teeth. "I didn't want to hurt you—"

"Do it!" she cried, her nails tearing deep furrows in my back, and my teeth sank deep, hot blood flooding my mouth as I drank greedily from her fount, fucking her harder, her body arching off the bed, her scream of ecstatic release tearing free a heartbeat before her muscles spasmed around my fingers and climax tore through me. I threw my head back, the rush of blood and rapture near incapacitating.

"Rowan..." My name on Lily's lips was a sound of completion, then repeated became a refrain filled with comprehension as her fingers touched my bloody face, and finally tears, though I was at a loss to understand them, coupled as they were with what seemed relief and an almost hysterical laughter.

"Lily?" I frowned with concern, pulling us both upright so that she straddled my lap. I framed her face with my hands, trying to look into her eyes, worried that some kind of madness was upon her.

"I know you!" She laughed, brushing at her tears. "And I'm not crazy! All this time I thought there was something wrong with me."

"Lily, what are you saying?" I shook my head, because what she was suggesting wasn't possible. She couldn't know me. Couldn't remember.

"It's why Rachel broke up with me—why I was crying in the coffee shop!"

"You were crying because you miss your lover." She was making no sense.

"I was crying because it was never enough! Because no matter how close we were, or how much she loved me, I always felt empty. Felt like something was missing. I was crying because I thought maybe I was broken...that maybe I'd never feel..." She fixed on me then, her eyes wide and bright with something akin to religious zeal.

"But you! I know you. I mean, I don't *know* you," she was babbling, "but my body knows you—your touch, the way you feel. You fill me up until I feel like I'm overflowing." She was kissing my face, over and over, stroking me with her hands, but cold dread chilled me to the bone.

"No." I shook my head, taking hold of her forearms and stilling her movements. "Lily—you don't know me—"

"But I do—"

"No!" I was off the bed before she could even register my absence, gathering my discarded clothes and redressing with haste. "You can't know me. You couldn't possibly." I didn't know if I was trying to convince her or reassure myself. The thought that she'd carried some kind of memory of me all this time—

"I know you're not human."

There was certainly no denying that. There was a beat of stillness and our gazes locked in the silence, her dove-gray eyes imploring me to tell her she wasn't crazy, and that I was the truth she'd been searching for. I couldn't.

"Rowan, please!" she cried. "Don't leave now, not when I've just found you—"

"Sshhhh..." I soothed, and I lay down again on the bed, pulling her into my embrace, stroking her back gently. "Everything will be all right, Lily. I promise." I hated the lie; how bitter it tasted in my mouth.

"You could make me like you. You could teach me. I could stay with you." Her eyes were so trusting, so innocent. She was offering me everything I longed for; only she had no idea what she was really asking. My heart ached with the impossibility of the situation.

"Rest now, Lily." My voice was low and melodious, my kiss tender on her brow. I held her as she succumbed to the compulsion, the tension slowly easing out of her body, and her eyes drifting shut. I spoke to her softly, my voice a thread of sound whispering to her subconscious, stealing her memory of our time together, erasing my presence from her life.

I left London that night. I had no destination in mind, only the half-formed notion that I had to leave, that maybe, if I went to another city, to another place, I could forget her. And so I wandered, and in time found myself on the North Antrim cliffs of my human childhood in Ireland, staring out at the cold waters of the North Channel, listening to the sound of angry waves breaking against the jagged rocks a hundred feet below. This had been my beginning, both in the literal and transformative sense, and it was here that I sought refuge, spending my days beneath the ruined castle that had been my ancestral home, and my nights thinking of things for which I had no easy answers.

How had she known me? For there was no doubt that she had. I had stripped her of her memories, and yet she had retained some elemental knowledge of our previous joining. I had taken her blood and she had recognized me—had welcomed me—and pleaded with me to stay. Was it possible that what bound me so tightly to her bound her in turn to me? Was there such thing as a soul mate, and was she mine? Did I even have a soul? Or were my kind truly damned? Meant to wander alone, never finding peace with another? I shouted my questions from the cliff tops, but there was only the howling wind and crashing seas, and neither knew the answers I sought.

At length, I determined that I would return to London, to Lily, one more time. Maybe I would find my answers there. I went first to her flat, and though she wasn't home, it was easy enough to gain entry. Lily's flat smelled stale, as though no windows had been opened in a long time. Her bed was unmade, and discarded clothing littered the floor. I wondered at these signs of neglect, but then I saw the canvasses—piled against the wall, on the floor, anywhere there was space—all variations on the same theme: darkness, shadows, rivers of red. And in all of them, something—no—some*one* perpetually out of focus: A curve. A whisper of form, of femininity. Eyes the color of a cloudless summer sky and hair as black as night. It was me. Lily had drawn me.

I left her flat as silently as I had entered it, heading to the only other place I could think to find her. The coffee shop was bustling at this time of night, students working on projects, couples talking more intimately over their warm beverages, a slew of solitary patrons engrossed in their laptops. I sat at a quiet table in a corner and willed all eyes away from me.

A door opened behind the counter, and I saw her. Lily exited the storeroom and deposited a cardboard box on the counter, then went about replenishing the various-sized stacks of disposable cups. My heart constricted painfully in my chest. She had lost weight these past two months, and her clothes hung on her too-thin frame. Her cheeks were hollow and there were dark circles under her eyes, telltale signs that she wasn't eating properly, and had known too many sleepless nights. She moved listlessly from one task to the next, oblivious to the worried glances exchanged by her coworkers. Lily was fading. I recognized it for what it was, having encountered many such people in my existence; those people who the romantics say are half in love with easeful death, and whom I had been more than willing to oblige.

I had resolved to leave her alone, resolved not to take her from her world and bring her into mine because I had wanted to do what was right for her. I'd wanted her to have a life filled with sunlight and beauty. A normal life. But what if I had been wrong? There was no warmth in her eyes, no happiness. Only anguish and despair. What if there was no "normal life" waiting for Lily? Maybe there had been, and I had changed that fate the first time we'd met. Or maybe our fates had been entwined all along; maybe everything *was* written by one hand only, and Lily was my twin soul. Could I take that chance? Could I hope for a future I'd scarcely dared to believe in?

Lily was in the midst of wiping down tables when she

happened to glance in my direction. Only her eyes, instead of passing over me unseeingly as had all others, focused on me; she *saw* me. Her cloth dropped from her fingers unnoticed and she stared at me like a man dying of thirst who sees the oasis, but who still has the sanity to know it may just be a mirage. Hope against hope burned in her eyes. She approached me slowly, as though expecting at each moment that I would vanish and she would be left staring at nothing.

"I'm sorry to bother you," she said when she reached me, tongue darting out to moisten her cracked lips, "but do I know you? Have we met?"

There was everything in this moment. Every possibility stretching into infinite universes. I drank in her face, the face that had haunted me, whose every line and curve would be etched into my heart and my mind for all of eternity.

"Yes." I said. "Yes, we have."

SCRATCHED

Ashley Lister

Let me in!" Vicky pounded her mitten-covered fist against the door. The sharp edge of her cries was blunted by the vast empty moor surrounding her. "Let me in, let me in."

Should she threaten to huff and puff and blow the house down? The idea forced a humorless smile to tighten her lips. The grin faded when she realized those words should have belonged to Jake. He was the one who should have been delivering the wolf's blustered threat.

Something distant howled into the night. The cry combined menace with melancholy in a way that made her stomach muscles clench. It had taken two hours of walking to reach the shack. The journey had been an arduous and uncertain trek across the moonlit darkness of the North Yorkshire moors. She felt disoriented, weary and wary.

During daytime the moors had a deserved reputation for their desolate, majestic beauty. They occupied more than five hundred square miles of sparsely populated hills, heather and

countryside. During the day the moors looked magnificent.
But nighttime was different.

Making the journey alone and on foot at night, Vicky thought
it had been like hiking through primordial foliage.

The cry came again. Closer this time: a tormented baying.

She hammered on the door of the shack with renewed force,
determined to rouse a response, anxious for the comparative
security of being in Jake's presence. "Come on, Jake. Open this
bloody door. It's freezing out here."

It wasn't quite freezing. It was cold enough so that every
syllable she shouted was turned into a ghost of white breath.
But it wasn't quite freezing. A circular silver moon hung in the
inky sky. It was a shiny button, tarnished with craters, rilles and
maria. The moon was as small and far away as someone else's
problems.

"Jake. It's Vicky. You have to let me in."

She raised her fist, intending to slam it again at the wooden
door.

With an asthmatic creak, the door swung inward. It left a
gaping black shadow in its wake. For the first time that evening
she wondered if she had been wrong to follow him. Her skin
prickled with goose bumps that owed nothing to the night's
chill. She fought the urge to step back from the threshold. Her
heartbeat raced.

"Jake?"

"I told you not to come."

The voice, as coarse as gravel, crept from the shadows. There
was something feral in the timbre that she had never heard
before. But she had no doubt it was Jake speaking from within
the coal-black depths of the shack. This was exactly what she
had expected him to say. He had warned her not to follow. He
had said this was something he needed to do alone.

"You shouldn't be here," he insisted. "I told you not to follow me."

"You told me lots of things. You told me you loved me."

"This isn't the time or the place for *that* argument. I do love you."

"I'm not buying into the werewolf shit, Jake. In this day and age I'm surprised anyone still buys into—"

A hand shot from the darkness.

It snatched her arm. Gripped tight. Dragged her through the doorway.

Vicky started to shriek in protest. It crossed her mind to resist—pull back, struggle, refuse or fight—but she had journeyed up to this remote shack to see Jake. If she pulled away now it would make a mockery of her arduous trek across the moors. Worse: it would suggest she'd bought into his delusion; it would suggest she too believed in werewolves.

The shack's door slammed closed behind her. She heard the groan of splintering timber being forced into some sort of latch. And then Jake's hand returned to her bicep, dragging her through the darkness, urging her toward the sepia glimmer of a distant light in the gloom.

"Jake!"

His fingers were talons. Claws. They hurt through the multiple cardigans and coats she had wrapped around her body before venturing to this chilly corner of the English countryside. She didn't want to think how cruel his grip could have been if she hadn't been protected by those multiple layers of clothing.

"You shouldn't have come here," he spat.

"You shouldn't have left our home."

"It was for the best that I came out here."

"Best for who?" she demanded.

"Best for everyone."

He pulled her into a room lit by a single guttering candle. The flame was long with tendrils of smoke trailing up from its tip. Its glow was barely bright enough to brush the claustrophobic walls.

She refused to let herself be intimidated. It was only Jake. He might be capable of hurting her emotionally. He'd proved himself capable of that. But there was no danger of him hurting her physically. No danger at all.

Her eyes adjusted slowly to the gloom.

A rumpled cot stretched across one cramped wall. A pile of hardback books littered the floor by its head. The titles included *Bisclavret* and *Guillaume de Palerme*. Vicky recognized the books as medieval werewolf literature. She exhaled heavily. The shack's windows—she assumed they were windows—were hidden behind vast, thick blackout curtains: blankets that shielded the room from any stray beam of moonlight. Saddened, she lowered her gaze.

The signs of Jake's insanity were everywhere.

The floor was carpeted with a mulch of green leaves and white berries. Mistletoe. Purple-petaled flowers were strewn amongst the mess on the floor. With a single glance she guessed they were either monkshood or wolfsbane. The species were similar in appearance and, according to the fairy tales of folklore and mythology, they were identical in their alleged usefulness for countering werewolf curses.

She blinked back tears of disappointment.

The center of the room was dominated by an unprepossessing table. It contained the yellow candle, the remnants of a loaf of bread, and a timeworn knife. Vicky figured the knife had been used to inscribe the crude pentangle that scarred the surface of the table.

She refused to sob.

With a different malady, Vicky knew, Jake would be at the stage where he was writing quotes from Keats on the walls or self-harming. She chewed her lower lip to stop herself from voicing the observation. She wanted him to leave the shack and return home with her this evening. He wouldn't entertain such a suggestion if she started mocking his beliefs. Even if his beliefs were ludicrous.

"Jake."

"What?"

Vicky wanted to blame the dim pallor of the light for the veneer of squalor that coated every surface. But she suspected the room's dinginess had little to do with the quality of the candlelight. She was standing on mulch in a vandalized, windowless shack.

"This is a fucking hovel, Jake."

"It's better than I deserve."

For the first time that evening she got a chance to glimpse his face. The familiar thatch of dark curls was characteristically unkempt. His jaw—solid and square—was shadowed by razor stubble. The scar that slashed vertically through his right eye sat livid against his wan complexion.

Vicky tugged the mittens from her hands. It was instinctive to reach out and stroke her fingers against his punished flesh. But she knew Jake did not like being reminded of his injury. Against her best efforts of willpower, Vicky's bare hand moved upward. Her cool fingertips brushed the ridge of badly healed skin. The scar felt hard and obscenely warm.

His hand encircled her wrist. With only a little too much effort he refused the comfort of her touch and pushed her away.

She stifled a sob. If she had given full voice to the sound it would have come out as a groan of despair.

The scar had been inflicted two months earlier. Jake had been rambling on the moors. The same stretch of moors she had just negotiated to reach the shack.

He had been attacked.

All the elements had been right to fuel his consequent werewolf fantasy.

There had been a full moon. The moors were burdened with a legend of local notoriety. The attacker had the strength of an animal; the cruelty and cunning of a human; and the anonymity that came with clouds across midnight darkness. The whole scenario would have been as laughable as a low-budget horror movie if Eddie, Jake's best friend and hiking buddy, hadn't been killed in the attack.

The local police blamed a vicious stray. There had been previous reports. There had been other attacks on sheep and livestock. The police concluded the investigation so briskly as to make their involvement darkly suspicious.

Jake had awoken in a hospital near the moors. Vicky was by his bedside. He had stitches where his right eye had once been. He had survivor's guilt where his best friend had once existed. And, it transpired, he had disturbed sleep and a growing obsession with the supernatural.

"I've been scarred by a werewolf," he confided to Vicky several days after the event. "That's how the curse is passed on."

"That's how the curse is passed on in movies and fairy tales," she argued. "It doesn't work that way in real life because there are no such things as werewolves."

It was a statement that had caused a rift. She refused to say the words this evening, knowing they would not help win Jake to her way of thinking. But she couldn't stop herself from thinking those words.

She took a steadying breath.

"Come home with me," she pleaded. "Come home with me now. Tonight."

"No." He shook his head. "Not tonight."

She opened her mouth to ask if this was because of the full moon and his investment in the werewolf myth. Because she knew that was his reason, she closed her mouth and left the question unasked. There was no sense in revisiting an argument they had both lost before.

She stepped closer, forcing herself into his arms.

Reluctantly, with a predator's wariness, he drew her into his embrace.

"I've missed you," she whispered.

Without warning he tightened his grip around her. Her breasts were crushed against his broad, powerful chest. The shack was filled with stale air but, standing this close to Jake, her senses were excited by other pleasing and more vital stimuli. She caught the fragrance of his perspiration: an earthy musk that never failed to remind her he was her man. She was warmed by the animal heat that radiated from his body. He bent to kiss her and his unshaved cheek bristled against her skin. She shivered with the thrill of being cruelly scratched by his nearness.

There were too many shadows layering the darkness.

But she didn't need to see events to know what was happening. She could hear the throaty growl of his need as he pulled her more tightly into his arms.

"I've missed you, too," he admitted.

The words were whispered between urgent kisses. First his lips touched her cheeks, then her neck. His nose brushed beneath her earlobe and she heard him inhale as though drinking in her scent and slaking an unnatural thirst for her essence. His arms remained firm around her body. For one disconcerting instant she wondered whether he saw her as his lover or prey.

Dismissing the idea, despising herself for buying into his delusion, she returned his interest and attention with equal passion. She writhed against him, yearning for him to satisfy the unbidden need that now rose in her loins. It was only natural to press her pelvis against the urgent thrust of his arousal. It had been so long since they were last together that she had forgotten his size was such a desirable asset. If the thought hadn't subscribed to his newfound belief in shape-shifters, she would have sworn he now possessed the ability to make parts of his body grow longer and thicker.

She killed that idea, fearful it could become compelling.

"Come home with me," she begged. "I'm parked at the bottom of the moor." She kept her voice light and tried to pretend the car was conveniently close: not a ten-mile hike through uncharted darkness. "We can drive to a bed-and-breakfast. We can grab a meal and a shower. We can get through this together."

As she spoke, she tugged him out of his clothes.

The shack was far from warm but, after her walk across the moors, she appreciated that it was sheltered from the bitterest of the night's elements. More importantly, although she wanted to get him out of the shack and back on the journey home, she also needed to feel Jake's naked body against hers.

Inside hers.

Since the accident a part of him had been missing from her life.

The thought of revitalizing their passion was intoxicating. Heated warmth spread through the inner muscles of her sex. She shivered with fresh longing. Vicky renewed her efforts to tear the clothes from his body while he reciprocated and tried to undress her. The shirt fell from his shoulders. The zipper of his jeans rasped in the near darkness as it was tugged down.

"Please come home with me."

He said nothing. Instead of words he stripped the clothes from her slender frame. His actions were a blur of frenzied efficiency.

Vicky had tried to protect herself from the elements by wearing layer upon layer. Now that idea seemed ridiculous and restricting as she responded to the need he inspired. Hurriedly she tried to bare her body.

He wrenched the coat from her shoulders. Then he pulled off the first of her jumpers. She fumbled with the buttons on her jeans while he tried to drag away a cardigan from above her blouse. Impatience and incompetence eventually had him ripping the fabric so the garments fell apart. She was left exposed and vulnerable for him.

The stiff tips of her bare breasts stood rigid with arousal.

Moist heat surged wet through her sex.

She kicked off her boots as she ripped the jeans from his hips. When her own jeans were wrenched away she effortlessly slipped out of her socks and panties.

As soon as they were naked, Vicky was back in his arms. She clung to him and basked in the physicality of his nearness. She traced the contours and sensations of his body, marveling at the way she had forgotten the sensory detail of his touch in the few short weeks since they had grown apart.

His muscle tone seemed leaner, more well-defined than she remembered. The flesh above the muscle seemed slightly more hirsute, bristling with swaths of thick hairs she couldn't recall stroking before. His caresses, previously as soft as silk, now scratched with an insouciant cruelty that came from the coarse calloused skin pads of his palms.

The revelations were nothing more than passing insights from the periphery of her mind's eye. Vicky refused to accept that they could support Jake's interpretation of events. Just because he was a little hairier than she remembered, it didn't mean he was a werewolf.

She breathed in the musky fragrance of his nearness. She savored the fact that she was once again in his arms.

He urged her toward the cot.

If he hadn't inflamed such tremendous desire, she would have resisted. She hadn't come to the shack with the intention of rutting on a filthy blanket. It crossed her mind, if she had come here with the intention of luring him out of the shack by using feminine wiles, she would be dressed in stockings and heels. Either that or she would be down on her knees, gobbling his cock like a cheap hooker, and keeping him on the point of climax until he agreed to her demands.

But this wasn't a crude bargaining of sexual favors. This was her and Jake. They were together again after his accident. They were building a life beyond his injury.

He entered her before they fell onto the cot.

He took her with a breathless urgency that went beyond longing or desire. There was no teasing or foreplay or lingering intimacy. The tip of his erection brushed her labia. There was an electric frisson of shocking excitement. And then he was pushing and pressing hard against her. Her body, yearning for him, yielded in an instant. She bucked her hips toward him. He was immediately sliding into her wetness. And he was filling her with his unfamiliar girth.

Theirs was a passion, she thought, that manifested itself as a brutal, animal need. Desperate for the release her body craved, she responded with equal hunger.

They pounded their loins together with furious haste. They were building to a satisfying rush of pleasure that was so wholly carnal it bordered on being spiritual. She began with her back on the cot. Jake towered over her. He stood between her spread thighs. His hands raked at her breasts. His calloused palms scratched sandpaper caresses against the stiff tips of her nipples. His hips bucked back and forth with frenetic haste as he plunged repeatedly inside her.

Vicky screamed happily.

But she wanted more.

She tugged herself away from him, ignoring the glimmer of hurt in his eye. Turning her back to him, presenting her rear as she knelt on all fours, Vicky urged him to take her from behind.

Doggie-style.

The name of the position made her wonder if this was a mistake. But, because Jake could fill her more deeply in this style of coupling, she balked at deeming it an error. The rounded swell of her buttocks molded to the curve of his hips. Their bodies blended together with the synchronicity of jigsaw pieces. His hands clutched her shoulders, fingernails buried hard against the soft flesh. His erection slipped much deeper into her sex.

Without effort, he thrust her to the pinnacle of orgasm. His thick girth filled her. His length forced her inner muscles to shudder with eddies of mounting joy. She was elated to hear Jake roar in response as his climax left him.

And his molten heat surged between her legs.

Thrashing through her orgasm, Vicky reached out for one of the blankets that hung from the wall. She gripped the fabric tight in her fist and steeled herself for another rush of satisfaction.

Jake held her with renewed ferocity. He dragged his nails down her back while his length repeatedly pulsed inside her.

Entangled in the moment, Vicky wrenched at the blanket. The sheet of fabric tore away from the window. As it tumbled to the floor there was an instant where she was staring up through a naked window. A silver moon beamed down at her from the night's sky.

It was a full moon.

The room was flooded by its brightness.

And then they were roaring together. Spasms of pleasure racked their way through her body with the impact of a violent assault. The release was so strong Vicky could feel her consciousness instantly slipping away. She drew a startled breath and fell into the blissful release of a fully sated doze.

As soon as her eyes closed she was in the middle of the dream.

She was running through the night, hurrying beneath the same silver moon she had just glimpsed through the shack's exposed window. The vital scents of autumn surrounded her. Her nostrils flared to fragrances that were earthy, fresh and dangerous. She was naked but unashamed, savoring the nocturnal chill as the coolness caressed her bare skin.

Jake was nearby. He was similarly unclothed and equally unashamed.

And, together, they chased across the moors.

The pleasure of running was almost as satisfying as the pleasure of the sex they had just enjoyed. Almost. The exertion was thrilling. The stimulation to her senses was intoxicating. She was enchanted by every fragrance. She was made drunk by the beauty of every partly shadowed sight. She was wooed by the thrilling music of the night. And she was enjoying all of this with her beloved, newly discovered Jake.

"There," he whispered.

She saw the sheep.

Understanding came over her with a rush. Jake grinned and nodded encouragement. He didn't need to say anything further.

She knew what he wanted from her. It was the same thing she wanted to do for him.

Without thinking—acting solely on her animal instinct—Vicky fell on the creature. There was an ovine shriek. The sound was lost beneath the guttural roar of Vicky's attack. And then she was biting and clawing her victim. The animal went down with a whimper of despair.

Jake hurried to Vicky's side. He began to help her devour the prey. She caught the rich scents of blood and pain as the new lust inside her was briefly satisfied. Together they gnawed and clawed their way through the sheep's flesh. Then they fell on each other with a renewed frenzy of lust. This time, Vicky knew she would not be so passive in Jake's arms.

She opened her eyes.

She had no idea how long she had been lying on the cot.

Jake had covered her with a coat. He had returned the blanket to the window. The candlelight seemed to burn brighter than it had before. He was wearing his jeans again.

Vicky blushed. She sat up, holding the coat firmly over her breasts. "I didn't mean for that to happen."

"I wasn't complaining."

"I want you to come home with me," she started. The words sounded plaintive and tiresome. How many times had she asked him that question? How many times had he refused? "Tonight," she added quickly. "You can come home with me. We can visit Doctor Etheridge first thing in the morning."

Jake shook his head. He had produced a bottle of brandy from one unlit corner of the room. She watched him wipe two shot glasses and place them beside the candle in the center of the pentangle.

"Tomorrow," he said. "Tomorrow, I'll return with you. I'm still not convinced it would be safe for me to leave here tonight.

But, unless you object, I don't mind sharing the cot with you if you want to stay until then."

He pushed a glass into her hand. His fingers lingered against hers. The subtle contact made her stiffen and regard him with renewed interest. It was only when he walked away that Vicky sniffed the contents of her glass.

It was befitting Jake's eclectic style that they were drinking an expensive cognac in a mulch-floored hovel. She toasted him as she nodded agreement to his suggestion. "Tomorrow we'll go back home and see your doctor."

And, as she sipped the brandy, she wondered if Jake's doctor might have a spare appointment for her. Her dream had been painfully vivid. Etheridge might be able to analyze what it meant. Even if he couldn't explain the cause, she figured he could give her some antibiotics and adhesive bandages. She curled a protective hand—the hand that wasn't holding her brandy—over her bare shoulder. Her fingertips touched the cut skin from where Jake had dragged his nails down her back during his climax.

The wounds were wet with thin rivulets of blood.

And, when she licked her fingers clean, she thought the coppery-flavored liquid was more intoxicating than the brandy.

BITTER AND INTOXICATING

Sharon Bidwell

É mile beheld the rough lines of age and labor in the hand
before him. The network of passing years bisected by a scar
and punctuated by torn cuticles threatened to entrap him in a
labyrinth of wanting. If only he could capture the essence of
that hand, the person it belonged to, in a drawing.

The hand lay upon his. He wanted to snatch back his fingers.
It felt as if that hand scorched him with disapproval. The other
hand held the promise of whisky. He wouldn't flinch from the
person whose job it was to pour it. Even so, he couldn't keep his
fingers from flexing, clawing, turning ugly.

"Émile, don't," the woman said.

"Another," he insisted.

She sighed, taking back her hand, using it to hold the glass
steady as she poured the amber solution to all his problems. If
only he could get drunk enough...

He tossed it back. "Another."

"I should cut you off," the woman muttered, refilling the

glass before moving off to serve another customer. Émile could tell by her tone she didn't have the heart to do so. She heard too many tales of woe to be so spiteful.

What was he doing here? He should be back in his room, working to complete his masterpiece. Art took sacrifice. He shouldn't move away from it except to defecate. To piss was easier. He opened a window and added his own libation to the aroma in the alley out back of his apartments off the Place Pigalle. People blamed the fragrance of ammonia on the cats and dogs, but it was the smell of human waste.

If only he could capture the waste of humanity. If it were impossible to recreate ecstasy, maybe he should depict baser feelings.

Émile stared down at the half-empty glass and turned his head looking for the bottle. Soon he'd need another refill.

It took him a moment to realize another hand was touching his. He looked down, dazed gaze following the passage of silken fingertips tracing lazy circles on his skin. The hand was feminine; skin smooth, unmarred; the manicure perfect; small daggers of scarlet threatening a rapture of torment.

The touch felt delicate. He suspected less delicate intent. He had no coin to spare and his cock... Émile almost laughed. His cock had wilted along with his talent. He looked to his left to see what manner of woman would dare to sit beside him.

Lovely.

The thought struck him as pointless but it demanded his attention. What manner of prostitute was this so perfectly preserved, so beautiful and pristine? Her flaming hair enflamed his heart, as well as parts of his anatomy so long shriveled they may as well have perished.

She smiled at him without flashing her teeth. Taking her hand from his, she picked up his glass.

No!

He almost reached for it, jolting a little in his chair, dismayed at his despair over the potential loss of his drink. If she took even a sip...

He had no cause to worry. The woman merely sniffed at it, pulled a face, and set the glass back down.

"This is no drink for an artist." Her voice, melodious, plucked wicked strings producing discordant notes in his being.

"H-how did you know?" he asked her.

Her lips pursed, drawing Émile's gaze to the perfect sketch of a cupid's bow. He longed to kiss it almost as strongly as he longed to portray it in charcoal, ink or oils. Almost.

"I always know. It's easy to recognize potential when I see it. When one knows what to look for, it's almost too easy. One succeeds...eventually."

A shudder passed through him. "I wish I could believe that."

"You need faith. Success is like a painting. It takes time and patience."

It occurred to Émile that this minx was manipulating him. He struggled to care. Turning away, he stared morosely into the glass, and then reached for it, tipping back his head to down the whisky.

Her hand blocked his, held the glass imprisoned an inch from his lips. "Don't," she pleaded.

Émile hesitated. "B-but I paid for it."

She relented. "Then finish it. Only...then come with me to savor a new experience."

Émile staggered, then leaned against the wall, closing his eyes. The taste in his mouth had soured. The cool night air hadn't helped as she had said it would. His stomach flipped over; his throat knotted. He refused to give in to sickness. He couldn't even remember making it to the end of the road, and he had no idea what street they'd finished on. His sole recollection was the sensation of leaning against this woman's curvaceous body, yet he remained detached from it. Even as she'd helped him up the stairs to her room, his head had lulled on her shoulder. Somnolent. Sleepwalking. Only the sound of his snoring had awoken him.

"Your name," he rasped out, clinging to the wall and the sound of his voice—normalities as an antidote, an aid to sobriety. "You didn't tell me your name."

"Vérène," she said, softly. Her voice tinkled. Was she making fun of him?

He didn't care. What difference did it make? So many laughed at his art and in there was his quintessence. There was only one reason a woman brought a man back to her room so quickly. She might have class, and he'd told her he had no coin, but either she didn't believe him or didn't care. He supposed he should feel flattered. He should fuck her; bury his self-loathing betwixt her creamy thighs.

"You're inebriated," Vérène said, and he almost laughed at the absurdity of that statement. "But not on whisky," she added, capturing his attention. Despite his self-pity, Émile turned his head to her.

She'd removed her cloak, revealing a luscious body barely concealed in a green diaphanous gown. The material seemed to float on gentle air currents as she moved across the room, her feet appearing to dance upon the bare boards. Beneath the filmy layers of her dress her body undulated. Pert breasts. Dark cleft. Enticing. Émile felt some surprise at his inclination to be persuaded.

Translucent temptation. Now why couldn't he paint *that*

instead of the crude display of a half-dressed female? He'd wanted to capture femininity, its grace, its strength and sensuality. Instead, he'd painted a grotesquery of woman. It struck him suddenly that what he couldn't see was as alluring as what he glimpsed.

"You need a drink." Her voice chimed, notes playing with his heart and mind.

"I thought I was inebriated." He had to be, to feel this way. He was not himself. He was a reflection only of what he wanted to be, indistinct, insubstantial. The morbid color of the room suddenly brightened, became a surrealist dream, gaudy and melting, disturbing. Sanity screamed with the piercing pity-inspiring cry of a mental patient. Émile swallowed. His throat felt dry.

Vérène beckoned, red fingertips and crimson lips emphasized by rosy nipples. Even through the green gauze, he could see those peaks pointing in accusation. It was as if they were things apart from her body, sentient, aware of his desire. Émile could feel the hard pebbles rolling against his tongue as if he played with them in reality despite Vérène moving ever farther away across the room. He dragged one stumbling leg in front of the other, following.

To his surprise, he spied a bar in the far corner. His temptress moved behind it and while she reached for items upon the shelves, he cast a quick glance around, taking in the brass fittings, the velvet covered chaise, the threadbare rugs, and the bed piled high with pillows. He staggered under the confusion of the room, a strange blend of poverty and opulence.

The glass she placed in front of him was slightly bulbous at the base, and made him think of an inverted teardrop. From there the glass flared out, though not widely. Into this, she poured a shot of liquid emeralds. Reaching beneath the counter,

Vérène brought forth a flattish spoon he could not deduce the use of; it had wavering slots in the base, the design a mimicry of flames, and would hold nothing. This, she balanced across the glass. Upon the spoon, she placed a sugar cube. Something stirred in Émile's mind.

"I've heard of this."

She looked up. Only then did he notice that her eyes were the same shade of green as the liquid. Pinpricks of light sparkled in these jewels and danced in merriment. "It's just a question of your poison. Ice-cold water or the blossom of fire. For me, fire. For you, I think water."

Drip. Drip. Drip. Émile didn't know how long he sat there, gaze flicking back and forth from the warm, slightly conde-scending smile of this vixen, and the water passing through the sugar cube to be displaced into the liquid beneath. The fragrance of herbs assaulted his nostrils, but he couldn't tell whether the smell came from the drink or from the woman. The liquid turned milky, as opalescent as her skin. His tongue itched to taste, but which should he choose? It had been long since he'd tasted the sap from between a woman's legs.

"Will I see monstrous and cruel things?" He'd read that somewhere.

Again, the curving of her lips seduced him. "Perhaps...on the first taste. Some things require sacrifice and perseverance, suffering. Those curious enough to be determined often see that which is wondrous."

"I would like to see wondrous things."

She smiled at him, and he instantly felt foolish for making such a statement.

"Tell me," she said, "about your painting."

"My..." His brow tightened in suspicion. "How did you know about my painting?"

Her gaze flicked up then down. "You don't have the look of a writer and there are telltale flecks of paint beneath your nails. Color is smeared upon your clothes. You're an artist. Tell me about your latest work."

"Y-you're interested?"

She leaned one elbow upon the counter, head on hand, gazing across at him from an angle, her body slanted, and one breast caught up on the edge and pushed forward, the ripe mound an offering. Émile couldn't stop his gaze from lingering. His tongue had swiped across his lips before he was aware of it. Turning her head and pursing her lips, Vérène blew softly over his mouth. His wet lips trembled under the cool breeze like leaves about to fall and as afraid.

"You're painting a woman?"

"Yes."

"Why?"

"Because of the subject..." He faltered, no longer sure of his reasoning. "I wanted to depict life. Women carry life within them."

"So does man." She raped him with her gaze. "I believe you chose poorly. What have you called it?"

It took him a moment to remember what they were discussing. "I...haven't... It's...no good. Useless!" He couldn't stop the sudden anger from exploding. "Pointless," he added, acidic bile in one sharp word. He might as well be talking about his life as the painting.

Red nails scratched a pattern of small scars across the counter. "What have you called it?"

"The..." He stopped. He didn't want to tell her but could think of no reason not to. Her attraction was a physical force that pulled him toward her, made him want to spill his heart's blood for one sweet kiss even if it polluted him. He glanced at the drink and tried to remember what he'd heard of it. Someone had said it was a depressant as well as a stimulant. He didn't know how that could be, but in some ways his feelings for Vérène were as ambivalent. Her presence calmed him even as he found his need for her alarming. Some drank to relax inhibition. Maybe he'd had too much to drink already; maybe...not enough.

"The essence of ecstasy." His voice sounded a long way off, yet simultaneously far too loud. "I-I don't think I can drink that. I've had too much."

"This drink is different." Her voice brooked no argument. "It will allow you to think logically. You're unhappy with your work."

He hesitated and then nodded, although he couldn't deduce whether that was a question or a statement.

"What if I were to tell you this would allow you to understand why?"

He lifted his gaze to her eyes and for a second believed he saw between the spectrum. The hint was brief, then gone. Her eyes were precious stones again, unyielding, unforgiving.

"What if I said this would not only allow you to see where you've been going wrong, but that it would clear your mind, allow you to see things logically. That it would break down the components of your painting so you would know how to connect each piece to create the essence not only of life but your entire being. The reality of human existence."

Words fell from her lips like silken pearls of semen in a nonstop orgasm. If she hadn't caught his attention already, the moment she spoke of essence, he was lost. "I would give... anything."

That smile again, a slow sensual twist of her lips, first tightening and then pulling to one side, promising to expose the white row of her teeth and then maybe the flicking tongue within, before twisting and closing almost cruelly. Her hands moved deftly, and as difficult as it was to look away from her face his gaze flicked down. His heart started in his chest at the sight of the knife, but not in an unpleasant way. The vision sped his blood, his heart pounded; the rhythm of his life sang in his ears. She pricked a finger and then held it over the glass.

"A last ingredient of my own design," she told him, eyes bright, and lips flaring to burgundy as she bit at them. He wanted to feel them cushion his cock in a tight band of marriage. A single bead of blood drew his gaze, hovering, seeming to hang indefinitely at the tip of her digit, and then...*splash*. It fell silently, deafening his mind. He could still see it, perfectly formed, a red teardrop suspended in the midst of the white cloud, beginning to dissipate. She held the glass out to him. He hesitated.

"It will give you new ideas," she promised.

"I've heard it makes a ferocious beast of man." He was surprised how strong his voice sounded, the strength of warning. He looked to her gaze, silently asking was she not afraid.

"I do hope so." Her choice of words taunted him, as did the way she spoke and the movement of her body. He stared at her even as she moved her hand, pressing the glass before him. The vision of her dimmed and blurred, until it shimmered, indistinct, and the glass and its drink became... everything. He took hold of it and drank.

"There now."

Soft hands petted him, coaxed, turned and spun him, pulled him. When his fogged mind cleared, he was standing just as he had been, and she had taken the glass from his shaking hand. He couldn't tell illusion from reality.

"What do you want?" She was mocking him.

He couldn't have her. He could sink his cock, but he couldn't *have* her.

"What makes you think that?" she asked. Had he spoken aloud?

"I want you," he told her.

"I know. And I you. But we both want something more."

He doubted her, but could not contain his anguish. "Yes. Yes!"

"You've not been able to capture it, have you? You want to understand, to explore the human experience. You want to portray it on canvas, show the demonic side of human nature and the angelic heart of humanity's potential. You want to examine the network within, what makes us human. Yet no matter how much paint you add to the canvas, secrets remain hidden and you do not understand. *We*, you and I, do not understand how humanity can stand to live without seeing, without *knowing*."

Beneath her nails the threads of his clothes parted, turned to shreds and the dust of ages. He vaguely acknowledged what was happening, but paid it little attention. Besides, it felt so apt. Everything in the universe was a particle of all and nothing. It felt right to be so naked, stripped of all pretense.

"How do you know all this?"

"Your mind is so open to me. So rich with thought and feeling. I could see it the moment I looked at you. A kindred spirit." She circled him, hands tracing the line of his arm to a bicep, capturing the muscle in her cage of fingers. Her flesh burned his. "You have no idea how long I have waited to find a man such as you."

"I know," he told her.

She chuckled. "Mayhap you do." She came around his other side to face him. Her hands still traveled, grasped him, *felt* him. "Yes, I think you do. You know all about longing. You called to me, begging me to show you the way. Nothing about you is closed to me."

"Nothing," he echoed.

She laid a hand on his rib cage. "Except the heart within your chest."

He shook his head. "Not even that."

"Yes, that."

"No." Tears threatened.

"No tears yet. You can stand more pain than this. You've endured more sorrow."

"The world is sorrow."

"Exactly!" The words hissed out, triumphant. "The suffering of the stranger on a street. The pangs of heartache and loss. The world cries out in silent agony, and only a few can hear it."

"No." He shook his head, his cock trembling in her hand. "You speak of only woes. There is beauty in the world and... and passion."

"A walking dream. A walking wet dream." He could hear laughter in her voice and couldn't tell whether her words were intended to soothe him or tease him. "Black atrocities of truth. Hopeless. You think this skin feels my touch?" She leaned close, whispered in his ear so that her breath stirred his hair, tickled both his neck and his ardor. "What would you feel if I reached inside you?"

"I-I don't...understand."

She pulled back, tugging his cock and then letting go so that it sprang to attention, slapped him in the stomach. "No way you could, but I can teach you. I can show you. Your work lacks life. If you come to me, you will have all the time in the world to get it right."

"All the time?" The woman talked in riddles, but he struggled to accuse her of any wrongdoing when she devoured him with her all-embracing gaze.

"Why not? Art is immortal, is it not?" She touched a fingertip to one pale pink nipple, no more than a pimple on his chest. "You're quite beautiful," she said as if surprised to discover this. "I like a sculptured torso and a weighty cock."

The heat of a blush traveled through his body.

"I never expected to find the talent I needed in such an artistic build. The musk of a man." She sighed, sounding happy as she kneeled before him, breathing in, her face an inch from his cock and testicles. "If I asked you to kneel in filth for me, would you do it? If I asked you to bleed for me, I wonder, would you?"

He hesitated, but in truth, he could give only one reply. "Yes," he said. "Yes, if it gave us both what we wanted."

"Oh, it will, it will!" Vérène promised, her hands spreading over his thighs. She gave kisses to his stiffness, treating him to tenderness. Émile wanted to thrust forward and force her mouth open, but knew she would not be rushed. Still, he could not help himself.

"Oh, please." His words were punctuated with the jolting of his hips.

"Such haste," she admonished with little torturous puffs of air against his overheated flesh. "Are you afraid of me?"

"No."

"What if I told you, you should be?"

The pounding of his heart told him to take a breath, to think. He ignored it. "No. Never." His cock twitched toward her lips in agreement.

"Never, my love. Never be afraid of me, even though you should be."

She rose. The gauze of her gown brushing over him was an abrasive scrape over flesh too sensitive to endure it, but endure it he did. She took his hand. He shook his head, confused. "I thought we…"

"Soon. So soon," she told him, one cool hand pressed against his face. "First we have work to do."

"A painting to create?"

"The finest. And the more you are aroused, the better the work will be."

He'd always considered arousal a distraction, buried it. He let her lead him, one hand on his wrist at first, and then drifting to his cock so that he stumbled a little in her wake. The shocks of pleasure and pain as she led him across the room made his balls swell with anticipation.

The canvas was larger than he expected. He glanced at Vérène with uncertainty. She looked down, her gaze tracing the sweep of her hand. "All you'll need," she told him. He blinked at the display of implements.

"All I...need?" Yes! As his hand took up the first of the instruments, he understood her meaning.

"I want to see a savagery of passion."

He nodded at her instruction and set to work.

His first strokes against the canvas were hesitant. He winced. "It hurts."

"I know. It's supposed to. One cannot portray only pleasure. Spread your legs."

His objection died on a spear. He obeyed her.

"Flawless," she whispered. Her fingers trailed over him, mimicking the red lines he committed to posterity. Her hands lifted and separated his derrière. He couldn't help it; despite the riot of color flying from his fingers to the picture, his muscles tightened. "Men," she laughed. "So sensitive about this one small point of entry. Well, you'll be touched and explored as I dictate. Isn't that what we both want?"

"Yes," he said, helpless, hands moving to make his mark for eternity. Fingers pried at him, made him cry out, but he never took his eyes from the slowly forming image.

"This will be an integral part of the painting," she said, a finger circling. "All of human experience, do you not agree?" He did indeed, even as his mind rebelled.

The pain came, breaking him open, leaving him strangely shivering with need. He tried to turn his head away, but she turned it back, pressing her lips to his, tongue flicking.

"This is what you've always wanted." She spoke, and he swallowed down her words.

"Such eagerness. Such greed. Work faster."

"Yes!" His hand flew back and forth in artistic endeavor. The slap to his backside made him lurch, distorted his aim and added the right stroke to the painting. "Again," he begged. She slapped harder. "Yes!"

Vérène chuckled. "I told you to have faith. There will be no mistakes in this masterpiece."

When the pain became too great, she soothed him with cool fingertips against his brow.

Vérène stood back, surveying the painting. "What say you?"

"Show me," Émile begged of her. She held up and tilted a mirror. A shudder passed through Émile, of pleasure that initiated a torturous shiver. "To think I never knew."

"And now you do."

"What would the critics think? Will they ever see this?"

"Yes." Vérène smiled that twisted smile of hers. "We'll travel together, and I will show the world your one creation."

"Just one?"

"No more is possible. Besides, how can one better perfection?"

"A critic called my last work the most basic of human desires. He didn't mean it in a good way."

She tilted her head critically. "All art is truth. Even when it's bad. The critic was an arsehole."

He giggled. She smiled.

"Speaking of..." She touched him intimately, inserted a finger. He writhed beneath her touch.

She kissed him deeply, and he couldn't resist the strong sucking of her mouth on his lips any more than he could her touch on any part of him. When she broke away, he asked, "Tears now?"

The question was redundant. His cheeks were already wet, but still he sighed with relief when she said, "Yes." He sighed from other emotions as she lifted his cock and balls, kissing his testicles, running her tongue over them. She mouthed his cock and finally let it past the barrier of her teeth. The contraction of her throat felt exquisite and Émile's cock swelled a little with pride at its own thickness.

Even as she sucked, he felt that tickling touch around his anus. She'd smoothed the way with some greasy substance. Émile strained his gaze but could not see what she had used.

"Close your eyes and concentrate on feelings," Vérène said, and he submitted. He knew what she was going to do even before he felt the nudge of the phallus.

He cried out, lanced, sharp jabs bringing nerves alive, as she plunged it deeper and deeper. Then she twisted the object, drawing it out so that the tip twirled, teasing the rim, before thrusting it back deep inside him. All the while, her cheeks puffed out, she sucked, her right hand clasping, tightening, riding up and down his cock as if, when he climaxed, she wanted to milk out every drop. Then moving her hand to gather up his balls, she bunched them up beneath his cock, increasing the angle for her mouth to sink right down, enveloping him in tight, wet heat. With her left hand, she stretched him open, using the fake phallus to make him yield. All the while, her head moved back and forth, tongue whipping his entire length, sucking when she reached the tip, before swallowing him again.

A thin, keening noise broke through Émile's stretched lips. He existed upon the rack, his body and mind stretched wide, his feelings elasticized. He wanted to thrust his hips forward, but could not do so. He wanted to push out his backside and impale himself for her amusement, but he was no longer capable of such movement. Vérène, his mistress, had him entirely at her mercy and it was...perfect. It was like the painting. He understood that now. Pleasure could not exist without pain and in the end both were agony; at last, his artistry was proof of this, and he was part of it.

His groans fractured in fierce spurts, spasms that sent colored sparks igniting behind his eyelids. His cries reverberated around the room and shivered over his naked flesh as though flames of fire licked his torn skin stretched to all four corners of the canvas.

It was deliciously terrifying, deliciously terrible.

Émile was not disappointed with his first review.

The Essence of Ecstasy strikes one as an exercise in contrast. The sculptured image of a male nude, captured in the peak of youth, is an allegory of violence, at once wholesome and noxious. It is depraved in its very narcissism and therefore, a work of perfection. One could accuse the artist of preening if it did not reach mythological heights in theme. Its underlying meaning multiplies until it drives out the insanity of its creation. It invokes reality in its very abstraction. The color and rawness incite a chill of such intensity that some have fainted in its presence. Others have fallen upon the floor moaning, humiliated in the throes of spontaneous passion. One cannot tolerate looking

*at it and yet once glimpsed, one cannot turn away and in that,
we have the essence of all that is human—the truth of all that
is horrible beneath the sublime. This work is possibly the finest
existing, showing humanity as both more and less than meets
the eye.*

"Happy?" Vérène asked him.

"Yes, my *déesse verte*," he told her, utterly content.

TEA FOR TWO

Claire Buckingham

He made the tea as he had always made it, strong and black. She watched from the kitchen table, hands demure and still upon the oak. The lack of conversation did not appear to bother him this morning, and so she was content to let the silence rest like a sleeping child between them. His eyes moved over the papers as he meandered his way through his toast, his jam, the ever-present pot of fragrant Earl Grey. To the left a second teacup stood empty. For a long moment she stared at it, remembering. Then, she sighed.

"I wish I could make the tea."

"Darling, I don't mind at all." She hadn't meant to say as much aloud, but he didn't look up as he rattled to the next page, took another sip. "You were never any good with tea, at any rate."

"No. I suppose I wasn't."

The teacup clinked against wood as he realized his slip, and he set it aside with the paper. "But that was not the reason why I married you." The words, gently given, were accompanied by the reach of his hand toward her. She watched it, unmoving. It stopped dead; with a wince, he drew back. The remembering had struck him hard and he turned to the window. The curtains were heavy with dust, drawn against the sun, but they both knew the great old buildings still lurked in the distance beyond the glass. "I should go into the university. There is much work to be done."

Drawing the housecoat tight about her shoulders, Anastasia watched while he folded the paper and set it upon the sideboard in its habitual place. He did not tidy away the remnants of his meal, and she made no move to do so herself. She trailed him instead to the front hallway, glum with its grand staircase and more of the interminable dusty windows. Morning light struggled to cut through the grime; what should have been a great rose window of scarlet and ochre and deep royal blue had become a sad facsimile of its former glory. Under its meager light her husband was scarcely illuminated. Anastasia herself might have been invisible until he turned and smiled at her with the quiet confidence she had fallen in love with years before.

"We are very close." As he thrust his arms through the sleeves of the greatcoat, she noticed how it had begun to hang loosely upon his frame. "It won't be much longer, I promise."

"Can you really promise me that?"

His gaze wandered back down the passageway toward the kitchen. She knew what he pictured, for she saw it so clearly herself: two teacups, one used and one empty. The rest of the set was carefully packed in newspaper in the attic. It had been a wedding gift. "For your family," her mother had said. "One cup to each." Anastasia's hand reflexively pressed to her abdomen. Gregory's eyes flicked toward her, catching the movement; he shook his head.

"The time for tears is done. We must go forward, never backward."

She bit back on the hypocrisy of his saying such a thing, though she followed him as far as the doorway. Caught at the threshold, she watched him go to the front gate. Once white as snow with the pink tea roses bright against the fresh paint, it had now become shabby, graying in the spring light. The gardens were no better, having suffered all the summer and the autumn and the winter; her roses were long since buried in graves of their own devising.

Sensing the weight of her gaze, he turned back as he placed his hand upon the gate and pulled it open. The hinges protested even this most basic of functions. But he did not leave her, not yet, though she stood alone in the shadowed doorway of the faculty house that belonged to that hovering hulk of a university.

The first time she had seen Gregory Moss, he had been then as he was now: haloed like an angel by early morning light. He had reminded her of the Archangel Raphael, the healer; she had thought that he would always make things better. Certainly he had done so, in those early days. In these late days, she wondered at her conviction, at the promises that echoed through the dusty corridors. The secrets of the university, properly unearthed, could rewrite the very laws of the universe. Or so he said. Anastasia had never known those laws in the first place.

When they had met, his gray eyes had always looked toward a world beyond their own. She still did not know where she had found the courage, because she had never been as brilliant or bright as one such as him—but Anastasia had brought him back down to earth, demanded he not leave again unless he took her with him. In his arms and at his side, both lover and wife, Anastasia had felt as if she'd voyaged through the solar system and beyond. She'd not understood any of it then. She didn't understand any of it now. In those days, everything had seemed only beautiful. These days were stranger, darker—and the space between them could have been the great span of that same universe, now cold and uncaring.

"Have a good day," she said, finally. "I'll be waiting for you when you return."

"I am sorry to always make you wait."

"I could wait forever."

"That is what I am afraid of." Only then did he look away, reminding her of the dusty subdued glass of the rose window; there was despair etched in every long line of his body, and her heart swelled with desperate affection.

"I love you." He turned back, startled. The movement brought with it the sudden memory of a Greek myth she'd read soon after first coming to this house, of Orpheus rising from the underworld and risking the look back just a moment too soon. She shivered, covered it with a smile. His returned grin was not of the old days, but it was enough. On impulse she blew him a kiss. One large hand snapped out, caught it with deft grace, then mock-swooned over the strength of her love. It was early, and no one could see their tableau. This was their private universe, bright and full of promise the way it had been before.

Then he turned away, walked away; he was lost to her for the long and lonely hours of another day. He always left so early for his work at the university now. She could not complain, knowing of other husbands who worked only for the drink at the end of it. Gregory's work had always been the most vital part of him—and these days his work was all for her. She should not complain. Not all husbands would be so devoted.

Yet the thought of the university, of the great old buildings and their grasping shadows, brought with it the irrational fear that the beast might swallow him whole yet. Anastasia knew such fear ought to be ridiculous. It was only a place of learning, no matter how odd a reputation it had garnered over the years. One could not blame the university for what had happened. Not even if her husband thought it might hold the unholy key to its reversal.

In a fit of pique, she slammed the door hard against all of it. But there was no one home to jump, for the housekeeper had not yet arrived. The glass in the rose window trembled. Somehow she could still smell the roses in the front garden, even though they were seasons dead. For a moment she considered running after him, barefoot, hair bannering behind her like the tail of a comet.

Then she turned, returned to the kitchen and the two teacups within. This house was her home now, and her place was within its walls.

Midday found her dozing in the master bedroom, filled with a yearning to go to him, to leave the shadowed house. The heat of the sun seemed far away, though she purposely lay in the part of the bed where it fell. Even when drenched in it she felt no warmth. Sometimes she felt as if she would never be warm, that she might never leave this house ever again.

"I was thinking of you."

Opening her eyes, she turned her head to find Gregory in the doorway. It was odd for him to come at such an hour, though she often lay on this bed and waited for his return. Sometimes she felt as if she'd never risen from it at all—sometimes she thought everything since that terrible summer day last year had been only fantasy. But he stepped forward, stepped closer, and he was no dream.

"Ana." In that one word she felt the strength of his yearning, as if it were the radiating heat and warmth of a birthing star.

"Are you not busy today, husband? You said that you would be busy."

She did not mean to put any reproach in her words. Yet he looked away, and she could see that they had stung. "I did not mean to disturb your rest."

"My rest is forever uneasy." The words were poorly chosen; she had to force away the thought of her name carved in marble, dated and stark. Instead, despite her lethargy, she forced herself to sit up. She had no right to exhaustion. While he went to that damned university every day all she ever did was wander the halls of the empty house, waiting for him to make the cursed elixir he had promised.

Then, he moved—already he was leaving her. Anastasia's heart sank, as did she. Though she would take the words back if he asked, they would both still know she had meant them. But he did not go, coming to rest in the dusty chair before the bed.

"Before I met you, I never knew the value of art," he said, soft and slow. "But now I go to the galleries, the sculpture annexes. The marble there, it intrigues me—how does man create such beauty out of such inert material? They might as well be alive."

"Perhaps they are, in a way," she murmured, but he continued over her.

"I cannot touch them." His eyes had turned distant, drifting toward the university. "I might only stand close, and watch. Their skin is luminous, like an invitation—and I, the moth to the flame, am helpless to do anything but draw ever closer." He paused, again. "It made me think of you."

"Am I a marble statue?"

"They look so real, as if a single touch could bring them to life." He raised a hand, skimmed it downward as if tracing the curve of her waist. "But I didn't want to see them. Not today. Not when I knew I had something far more beautiful, and infinitely more precious, all to myself." His eyes moved to the window. "*Touch*. I want..."

"What do you want?" The scarce whisper made him smile, sad and sorrowful.

"I want only you."

Without a word she loosened the belt about her waist. A moment later, she lifted the dress over her shoulders. The slip followed, as did the underwear beneath. Only then did she rise, standing before him in nothing but her skin. Perhaps she should have been too cold with the window open. It was spring, but the weather had not warmed. Yet under his gaze she felt the heat begin to rise at last.

"Just as you were," he said, hooded eyes hazed with memory. His exhaustion was more readily apparent in the noon light than it had been closer to dawn. She sighed. The work of his days was leeching his life from him. She wished again that he would stay back from the university. Stay with her.

"Would you like some tea?" She allowed one hand to move downward, to rest lightly upon one hip. His eyes followed as if magnetized.

"I will have some at the office."

She shook her head, prayed that he would not go. "I will make the tea for you again, one day." If she kept saying it, perhaps she would believe it. He only smiled.

"I will look forward to it." One hand moved back through his hair, dropped to loosen the stock of his shirt. "Even if it tastes of salt and sand, I will drink every last drop. It will be as an elixir of life."

She smiled, tremulous. "You do me too much credit."

"Then perhaps I shall take it for myself and make it true. For you."

His eyes still echoed her hand, resting upon her skin; she felt the weight of his gaze as if it were a true touch and shivered beneath it. But, exhausted as he was, he only observed from the chair. It was as if she were indeed the statue he had compared her to.

I cannot touch them.

In his place she allowed her hands free movement over the smooth planes of her skin. Perhaps he felt like angels did: watching the world below while forever unable to be part of it. Pushing aside the sadness, she curved her hand and cupped one breast. A flick upward, and the palm skimmed over the nipple, bringing it to startled life. In a moment, it was as hard and unyielding as that of any marble muse locked away in a gallery.

"Shall I?" she whispered. He swallowed hard and nodded. Her hands moved again, and it had begun; in an echo of her motion, his hand drifted downward. There was no fabric in her way, thus his hands paused a moment, the longer fingers working at his flies. Then they slipped beneath, and his whole body vibrated with the relief of true touch upon his heated skin.

"Think of my hand on you," she whispered. "As I think of yours on me."

And the memory of his long fingers gently tracing archaic patterns of life and death upon her deepest center brought her to another kind of life; the damp folds beneath her fingertips had filled with a tingle of familiar longing. It was not the first time they had done this, with him there and her here, but she wondered even as she traced a slow path how it was possible. She felt so alive. It should not be this way.

But with his eyes on her, and his clever fingers moving in slow invitation over the thickening length of his shaft, she cast aside the practicalities of their situation. That was reality. This was fantasy, and again she imagined his fingers on her skin even as they brought his own sex to flushed life, like a sun beginning to rise.

She thought of gravity, felt as if she was breaking free of its constraints, feathering her fingertips against herself. He had always been the master at this, the deep dance of fingertips both inside and out—but he had also been an ever-patient teacher. She had always taken a deep and curious satisfaction in the sensation of a second hand echoing the movement of her own. But his hand had been larger, had moved deeper. Now her hand quested alone—yet with his eyes upon her, she could still feel the familiar ghost of his guidance.

One fingertip brushed that small place, that secret place he had first shown her. With a smile, she met his gaze, pressed hard against it. Her sudden exhalation was echoed a moment later, and her smile dissolved into a low moan. Again, she pressed against that fount of sensation, eyes fluttering closed. Her legs could not support her. Like an angel falling from heaven she slowly descended back into the bed, onto the white sheets that had been washed clean of all dark red memory. Yet even had she wanted to think of that dreadful afternoon, this was no time for memory. It was instead a series of moments, a time of immediacy and urgency as her fingers moved, dancing until nothing else remained but his breath and hers, rising and falling in the dim dusty afternoon light.

As the end drew near, she felt the familiar sensation of the universe compressing upon them both: climax always left them alone and together at the center of everything when he was inside her. He was not inside her now—but as two, then three fingers moved deep inside her, it was almost enough. The thumb brushed, then pushed hard against her swollen center; she gasped, arched her back, the other hand clutching tight about the small swelling of one breast. As if from a thousand light years hence, she heard a second gasp. Her head fell sideways, eyes opening even as her fingers worked relentlessly on. His eyes had never strayed, fixed on her alone as his hand stroked in a rhythm like the harmony of the spheres.

"I want only you." The whisper was as powerful a stimulus as the hand that skimmed down her belly to join its twin at the juncture of her thighs.

"I know it." Something like salt water sheened his eyes; his hand skipped a beat, like a flickering far-distant star. "I cannot ever be without you, Ana."

Is that why I am here still? she thought suddenly. *Is that why I am here and our child is not?* And the university came to her mind, unbidden: dark buildings caging slender white bodies within. Her hands stilled. Then she looked to him and saw his hand moving with true purpose—hers picked up the rhythm, resumed the dance. In a joint symphony of touch they played skin against skin; separate celestial bodies at opposite ends of the universe, they moved as if in total eclipse, all shadow and light before the utter completion of their inevitable union. Anastasia came first, her back rising like a bow from the white sheet beneath. Her eyes closed again, deep in the darkness of her ending upon the bed. Memory hovered on the edges of her half-conscious mind, a black hole that threatened to consume everything left of her in this world.

Then she heard the choked cry. Her eyes flew open as she turned, saw him hunched over with eyes downcast. For a dreadful moment she thought that he *was* crying. Then he looked up and though it held sadness, his smile burned as bright as any supernova.

"Perhaps this is why they won't let me into the museum anymore." He sounded almost rueful as his gaze dropped to his palm, to the fading promise of life cupped within it. Her eyes widened.

"You *didn't*."

"No." His eyes met hers again, clear as the spring sky beyond the dusty window. "The need for touch, it's... I want you. Only you."

She napped after he had gone. She slept so much of the day and for most of the night too. But at least in the night she had the nearness of his warm body to take comfort in. During the day she had nothing but his memory and a dim sense of coldness that only seemed to grow with every passing afternoon.

The sound of people in the house brought her back to the waking world. With a frown she went to the landing, found the housekeeper and two others standing in the dim light of the rose window. The small man she immediately recognized as the dean of her husband's department. The woman, she did not. Beneath her great hat and wide glasses she was a silhouette, a Parisian fashion plate foreshortened by distance. As if reading Anastasia's mind the slim woman swept off the hat, the glasses; their absence revealed perfectly coiffed hair and a disdainful expression.

"Why is it so dark in here?"

"Dr. Moss prefers it that way. An ambience, perhaps?" The housekeeper's reply was weak. The smartly dressed woman rolled her eyes, keeping her gloved hands firmly away from the withered flowers upon the hall table.

"I shan't keep it that way myself." Leaning down to examine the flowers closer, she tsked, shook her head. "And it is so dusty! How does one even *breathe* in this mausoleum?"

Mrs. Taunton was affronted. "I do try, Mrs. Livingstone. But Dr. Moss, he is so very fussy. He...likes to leave things as they were."

"And the house falls into ruin around him," the woman observed. "Such a dreadful waste."

"Such a *pity*," Mrs. Taunton corrected, a wealth of untold

history in her words. Yet the woman had already turned back to the dean, adjusting her kid gloves with efficient purpose.

"Will Dr. Moss be leaving soon?"

"It has taken some convincing." To his dim credit, the dean almost looked ashamed. "He...is very fond of this house."

"It is so dreary," she insisted, "and yet...I could make it so much more. Yes, Dean Yeager, I think our family should be very happy here. We shall move in as soon as feasible. No need to see the rest of the house now, I have other appointments, but..."

She had more to say—Anastasia had the impression that Mrs. Livingstone was a woman with much to say, always—but she turned, looked briefly upward. Anastasia felt her heart stop—for it was as if she had seen her standing there, a white shadow upon the landing. Yet Anastasia may well have been a pane of glass: the woman looked straight through her, and then looked away. As the three left through the front door, she did not look back.

Anastasia clattered down the stairs, ducked her head to peer through the dusty panes that framed the heavy front door. The gate closed with a mournful screech, ending the dirge-like rhythm of the woman's heels against the cracking tiles of the path. The dean waited for her on the other side, and then they moved off together, in step, away from the house, and away from Anastasia. She closed her eyes, and wished she still had strength enough to cry. Yet she stayed silent as the grave.

Evening shadowed the sky with gray when Anastasia noticed the vague scent of cooking food, though she had not cared for such trivialities in many months. She instead remained upstairs in the great master bedroom, anticipating his return. Dusty and half-abandoned as the room was, her husband still slept there every night. It was more than could be said for some, she knew. Yet he so very rarely entered it by the light of day.

Upon the bed, Anastasia recalled the earliest moments of the afternoon: then, she had been as a marble goddess waiting for her god to descend, to bring her back to gasping, grasping life. It was such a different memory from those that came before it in this shadowed room. Her hands moved over her breasts once more, and she sighed. Though small and firm now, she remembered the days when they had filled with milk, heavy and pendulous with the promise of her body, and of his. She then recalled the dean's words on the day they had walked into this house with the bright hope of a young couple in love with both life and each other.

"It is a house for a family," she murmured. "Children should fill these halls with laughter."

She left the room and its whispering, wailing memories to descend again to the ground floor. She would go outside, she decided. She would look at the trees and the flowers, then the weeds and the waste, and plan how she would make the garden bloom again. She could not grow proper tea here. But there was always jasmine, mint, other herbs. Perhaps with them her tea would be better, when she had drunk the promised elixir of her husband's labors.

Yet as she looked at the dead and dying garden, she wondered at his promise, at the unspoken cost. The early days of her pregnancy had also cost her; from the beginning Anastasia had suffered for the gift, the second life within her own taking so much from the first. So much of her time had been spent on the daybed in the morning room, or on the seat upon the porch, unmoving as the seasons changed all about her. But she had not begrudged the child its needs, and neither had Gregory—then.

She laid her hands over her abdomen to find it flat, empty of life. Just another memory, half faded in the web in which it had become entangled. A strange desire to see the skin welled up within her. Lifting the dress, the slip, she found only white skin beneath. Unmarred by scars, ignorant of all memory, it made it seem as if those days had never been. She pressed her palm hard against it. Had any classical sculptor ever brought to life the form of a mother and child, while the infant still slumbered within? Or would that be too much life in something with none?

Letting the dress flutter down, Anastasia drifted inside, thought perhaps of reading until his return. Gregory had often brought her books from the library as she had grown larger; they'd spent many hours with those books on the daybed, on the porch swing. His hands had rested upon her as she read, feeling the life within. So many of those books remained within the house, never returned. Sometimes she looked at them and shuddered. Where once they had been a mere curiosity, fascinating in their obscurities and outright obscenities, now they were like lurking creatures of the dark just waiting for their moment to strike. Yet even in those lighter days she had thought them strange—if then only harmless.

"Why does such a sensible place have such arcane works?" she had asked him. "Surely the chaplain, at least, would think such books of no use."

"It is a strange place. I haven't told you the half of the peculiar things I have heard."

"But really," and she had pointed to the page of his latest acquisition, "life beyond the veil of death? Of course there is such a thing, we shall find our salvation in the arms of our Lord, but this..."

He had read over her shoulder of the dark bargain, eyes creased in thought as he examined the words of the grimoire. *"To reverse a death, all one needs is one life given for the other....* Well, perhaps that is not so odd, Ana. It is the balance of the universe."

She had craned around, fixing her eyes on his. "No, it is the power of a god."

"Well, then one should hope those who stumble across such power would but use it wisely," he had said, negligent, one hand warm on her belly; she had shaken her head.

"Thank god we have no use for such a thing."

"Thank god," he had murmured into her hair. The hand had then moved downward, seeking the warmth beneath the great curve of her abdomen. "But then, do you not feel as if you were a god, or a goddess, creating life in this way?"

She had smiled into the curve of his lips. "That is God's gift."

And he had held her close, his fingers questing beneath the thin veil of silk between his skin and hers before pressing his fingers deep within her welcoming warmth. "Then it is one I am glad to receive, again and again and again."

He had been able to touch her, then. But in those days they had never known a world any different. The university's strange secrets had not mattered. The house, a gift of that place, held no power over her body, over his mind. Alone in her flowering garden, shielded from prying eyes, he had raised his other hand and pressed down the fabric of her bodice. The cool night air had ghosted across her bare breasts for only a moment; he had then pressed his mouth against her collarbone before tracing a path downward. His lips against the stiffening nipple had been warm, and a touch of teeth had made her shiver. She had thought of a nursing child, but he had been stronger. And the fingers still deep within her had been stronger still, moving deeper with the unerring forward momentum of a comet.

It had been awkward, with the swelling of her belly between them. But she had aided his need, moving the dress upward as he turned her. She hadn't been able to see his eyes as he drew his fingers away. Then the warmth of his member, his most vital part slipping deep within her, made their connection as vital, as real as the life within her womb. He had thrust hard, as if seeking to move within her; with one palm still on her breast where his lips had lingered, he could feel her quickening heart-beat. She had, as always, come utterly alive under his knowing touch. They had not been two separate bodies orbiting the same sun. They had been as one, for death had not yet dropped the veil of different universes between them. Not then.

With a great sigh Anastasia closed her eyes and lay back on the bed. She felt as if she had been lying there for a very long time. They had moved her body. It rested now beneath a loving duvet of flowers and dirt. But her spirit had never left this house—and thinking of the day's visitor, she wondered if it ever would.

Later, she went out to the porch to meet him. It had been their tradition: he would come home and they would sit together until it grew cold, or until dinner was ready, or until it was too dark to know each other except by sound and touch. Their first summer had been rich with the scent of the gardens she had nurtured since their arrival. Now it was all shadow where it had been light, the rich scents a false memory in the overgrown garden. On the table between their chairs, though there were still two teacups, the tea had been poured only for one.

"I was thinking, today, after you had gone."

He looked up from examining the contents of the teapot. "Oh?"

"I...liked it. That you came to me. But I simply... I just..." She kept her eyes on the glimmering horizon, the jagged skyline of the sprawling university half hidden by the overgrown trees. "It's not enough."

"No." His hands stilled, his face etched in profile by the setting sun. "It never is."

"But then maybe it's already too much."

Her murmured despair startled him. "What do you mean?"

"This should never have happened."

"No," he said, firm in his conviction. She knew he thought of the marble carved with her name, buried now in a nest of dead flowers, and she shook her head.

"Not that. This." She waved a hand, encompassing the universe. "I shouldn't be here."

"But you *are* here. And I won't let you go." She wondered if he knew about the woman, even as he said urgently: "I am so close, Ana. It will be done."

"On earth, as it is in heaven," she finished, dark and low in the encroaching chill of evening. "But do you ever think of him? Of Isaac?"

For a long moment he was silent; perhaps she had hit too close to the truth. Then his face creased in pain, and he looked away. "There will be others, Ana. There is no need to consider such things now. It is only a matter of balance. The boy—"

"His name is Isaac."

"He has no need of a name." His hands spasmed, as if dying to reach for hers. She'd always been eased by his touch, whether upon her own hands, or deep within where the pleasure blossomed strongest. "Ana, *please*. It will not be for much longer."

"I cannot stay here." She looked to her own hands, pale and bloodless now; his eyes told her that he did not know. "Do you remember what the Dean said, in the beginning? It is a house for children. For a family."

"There will be other houses, Ana. There will be other children."

Only if you exchange one life for this other, she thought, and shook her head. "Do you ever think it is not our place, to decide such things?"

"If there is any sin, Ana, it will be mine." One hand moved, as if he would touch her arm, her shoulder in comfort. Then he remembered, and his eyes creased in pain as he looked back to the tea. "But how could it be a sin? It is love that keeps you here. And it is love that will bring you back to me."

But wasn't it love, that brought our son to us? What of that love? Turning her face to the sky, she realized she did not even know where her son laid his head. But should he look up, he would see the same stars beginning to emerge from the deeper sky. The thought might have comforted her, had she not known that those same stars shone too upon the damned university. Did those stars care about what dark things they shed such scant light upon? Her husband bent his head again to the tea, and she felt only despair.

"I wish we had never come to this place."

Gregory glanced up, having only half heard the scarce murmur. "What was that, my dear?"

"Nothing." She looked to her still white hands. "I said nothing."

He made the tea as he had always made it, strong and black. Then he drank deeply. Anastasia could see the beginnings of age in his eyes now, but the beat of his heart remained a strong pulse, shadowed in the hollow of his throat.

"Soon, my dear," he repeated. "Soon we will drink tea together again."

Yet tonight her cup stood empty. Anastasia remained motionless at his side, staring out into the garden. He had never cared much for her plants, her trees, her flowers; the overgrowth had only become worse with this, the second summer. The weeds pressing up toward the house were like the greedy grasping hands of time itself.

When she chanced a glance to her side, she found him smiling into the distance. If she parted the overgrowth of tree and bush she would find the damned university waiting for them: darkly dreaming spires, bright with their false promises of love beyond life and knowledge without the lesson. Yet even though the veil between them meant she could touch him no more than he could touch her, she had felt him that afternoon. She felt him still, and knew that whatever else came to pass between them there would always be love. Even if it twisted and darkened to match the Gothic spires of the clock tower to the west, there would always be love.

"And that is the tragedy of it," she whispered.

"What is that, Ana?"

"I am just thinking of the tea." When she opened her eyes she looked into the heart of the setting sun, and did not feel its burn or its loss. It would only rise again tomorrow, and perhaps that would be the day he would be forced to leave while she remained. She looked to the table, where there had this night been only tea for one. *Is it a betrayal, husband mine,* she thought with one hand resting alone on her flat dead abdomen, *that I should never again want there to be tea for two?*

MILADY'S BATH

Giselle Renarde

No sense asking me why she does it. Why scamper out the window every time the moon is full? Why flee the comforts of a warm feather bed knowing she'll return with her gown tattered and her flesh torn to shreds? Like I said, I'm not the one to ask. I've never lusted for any man, and certainly not with such hearty devotion as Milady lusts for that beast she seeks to tame. If ever I had sought the rough touch of man, I might understand why she puts herself in harm's way every second fortnight. If my inclinations were anything like hers, I wouldn't be so quick to judge Milady. I also wouldn't be so quick to run her bath on those nights she returns from the forest wounded but happy as a meadowlark.

She wakes me by the rustle of her skirts if I've fallen asleep, but it's rare I should slumber on the nights Milady sets off into the woods. I worry about her something dreadful when she's gone away. And I always know when she's gone because, though it in't the custom with proper folk, I end my day in Milady's bedchamber.

Most girls who work in great houses share sleeping quarters with other maids. Those lodgings are far away from the family's own rooms. I am far luckier than all those other chambermaids and servants. Me, I share a bed with the girl I adore more than anything else in the world: Milady, my love.

Ever since she was young, Milady had a wild streak in her. She was always chasing after the boys, and the boys had a name for her I'm sworn never to repeat. The Lord and Lady, her ma and pa, traveled the world over without the poor girl. They often visited the continent and even ventured so far as India and Africa. I don't know what they were looking for in all those countries out there, but it seemed to me they'd have been just as happy staying home with their daughter.

When Milady grew into adulthood, her ma and pa tried to make her prim and proper like themselves, but she wouldn't hear of it. She loved young men below her station, and none of her parents' persuasions would change that. The Lord and Lady then enlisted my service. I was 'round about Milady's age, always a shy girl, but a polite and modest maid. Also, I never broke vases like our Rose always managed to do, and I didn't cover up the bits on the garden statues with old burlap like our devout Auntie Dorcas.

When the Lord and Lady of the manor instructed me to report on their daughter's comings and goings, I gladly took up the task. Milady was less than thrilled, at first, about the maid sleeping on a cot in her chamber, but before long she did summon me into the big bed. The Lord and Lady expected me to temper her rotten behavior, but that in't at all what happened. If anything, my being there made her even more unruly.

And then this madness with the creature began. It weren't quite a year ago she started sneaking off in the night to meet him. Who this beastly man might be, I haven't a clue. Some sort of nomadic ruffian, perhaps? Or a convict who escapes his prison cell once every month? All I do know is that every time the moon is full, Milady slips out of bed thinking I'm none the wiser. She steals the same blessed frock out from the back of the wardrobe and pours it over her silk underclothes. At one time, she'd looked a dream in that velvet gown the color of fine red wine. Now the fabric is torn from the skirts to the sleeves, and the hems are caked with mud.

When Milady's gown was new, it had a décolletage of lace that climbed all the way up her thin neck and was secured at the nape with pearl buttons. The lace is gone now. I lay a bet that rakish fellow couldn't wait to get his filthy paws on what was underneath and tore the lace clean off. Now her pale breasts cling to the edge of her constrictive bodice as though they might leap out at any moment. And, though I have seen Milady unclothed on many occasions, my pulse always races at the possibility of more.

I do wonder what he looks like, this rake of Milady's acquaintance. He must be devilishly handsome if she returns to him month after month. Could an ugly man tear a woman's fine apparel to shreds, leave her body bloodied and broken, and still compel her to return at regular intervals? The thought defies imagining. But, as I've said, I am not like her.

When she is dressed in her rags of velvet, Milady tosses a hooded cape over her shoulders and slips out her grand window. Desire is the only force that could compel her to climb down the stonework like an experienced mountaineer. Only when I hear her feet touch the ground do I jump out of bed to watch her race through the gardens and off into the clearing. I lose sight of the cape concealing her long orange hair when she scampers into the woods, fearless as a tiger but vulnerable as a hare. Sometimes I think the girl acts solely on impulse, and how I envy her for it!

As I await her return, I imagine what sordid acts of carnality she dares to engage in with her brute. When we are alone, Milady and me, I am tender with her body. I curl in against her and wrap my arms around her willowy form. She allows me to explore beneath her nightclothes, and I caress her breasts with the gentlest of hands. My fingers traipse between her thighs and dance in the pool she creates just for me. Her arousal stimulates my imaginings, but I can imagine no greater happiness than lying in bed with my love.

Milady's monster of a man is anything but gentle. His rough treatment is apparent in each incision of her flesh, every bite and every scratch. He devours her breasts until each perfect pink nipple is swollen and red. Clawing at her back with razor-sharp nails, he gnaws on her flesh, from her soft bosom to her shoulders. Only when he is satisfied with the damage he's done to her top half does he tear up her skirts. He searches for warmth between her legs.

He is brutal with her, and somehow she appreciates this quality. Perhaps he throws her to the ground so her face meets the dirt and decay of the forest floor. Perhaps he pins her up against a tree so her naked breasts are further tortured by jagged bark. I can scarcely imagine what pleasure she might derive at being impaled from behind by a hulking creature of the night. Certainly he forces himself upon her; she returns home dripping with his seed.

I imagine the expression on Milady's face when he enters her body with furious force. Wincing, she grits her teeth and shuts her eyes. I wonder if the act pains her. If it hurt as badly as I presume, she would never return to him. Indeed, no woman would enter into carnal relations with any man. My fingers know the wetness her desire inspires. If only she appreciated the ardor of my love, she would stay in bed with me rather than venturing out to the woods in the middle of the night. Perhaps my kind hand is insufficient to her purposes. It's possible she savors the sting.

When I catch sight of Milady stumbling out of the forest, I hop back into the bed we share. Under the covers, I wait to hear her footfalls in the garden below and then her whimpers of exertion as she climbs the old stone wall. The window hardly creaks as she opens it wide and moves through like a specter. Only when I hear the rustle of her skirts do I sit up in bed and rub my eyes as though I had been sleeping all this time.

"Ah, you have ventured out," I say as she casts off her cape. I observe the state of her gown and sigh. It has been torn anew where I stitched it up last month. The front of her bodice hangs open, her naked breasts scarcely concealed by underthings. Her nipples glow pink through dirty white silk. The scratches across her ravaged chest are red and raised, but her wounds are not bleeding tonight.

"I have ventured out," she finally concedes. When Milady runs her fingers through her tangled hair, twigs and leaves and all manner of things fall to the floor. "But now I have returned and I shall require my bath forthwith." She wipes dirt from her cheek, but it persists. Her hands are as muddy as her face.

I slip from out of bed and throw a shawl across my shoulders. Bowing ever so slightly, I reply, "Yes, Milady," and tiptoe from her chamber in my simple cotton nightdress. Cook ensures the stove is always lit, and water always upon it for those who wish a cup of tea late into the night. I replace the two kettles I've taken before leaving the kitchen. The hot water steams as I climb the darkened staircase, quiet as a mouse though my arms shriek with pain. This task is an onerous one, but there is nothing I wouldn't endure for Milady.

When the lengthy preparations for her bath are complete,

she disrobes slowly, dropping layers of torn velvet and then silk to the ground at her feet. Under the dim light of wax candles and oil lamps, I observe her naked flesh marred by scratches and bites. Her pale belly, chest and thighs have been clawed as if by a biblical beast, but when she turns her back to me I am most frightened of all. "You're bleeding, Milady! And it in't time for nature's curse."

Stepping into the bath, Milady offers a secretive smile that makes me feel foolish. Spreading her cheeks, she looks over her shoulder, but I doubt if she can see the blood and seed dripping from her backside. Those fluids trickle slow as molasses down her thigh, but my eye cannot escape the image of her tortured bum hole, if you'll pardon my French. The sight turns my stomach, and I clench my buttocks tight as I'm assaulted by the vision of what that beastly man did to my lover.

"Bugger," Milady says. Her voice is light as a meringue. She seems amused by all that's happened and proud of it as well.

"Does it hurt, Milady?"

"Indeed it does, dearest Bet." She clutches her cheeks with dirty fingernails. "Like a hundred knives shoved up my arse."

Milady winces as she glides into the bathing tub and dunks her head under the water. Her soft breasts float to the surface even before the tip of her nose rises up. Her wet hair emerges and she gasps for breath. All else but her scraped knees remains underwater.

Seating myself on a cushioned stool at her side, I soak a square of cotton in her fragranced water and wipe the dirt from her face. She smiles at me as though we shared a secret, but I must admit it's a secret I don't fully understand.

"Have you truly never been intimate with a man?" she asks. "You can confide in me, dear Lizzie. I promise never to tell a soul."

Shaking my head, I run the cloth down Milady's smooth neck. The white cotton turns gray and I must start again with a new square. "I regret I have nothing to confess. I have no desire to be intimate with any man."

She hisses when I touch the cloth to her chest. Her scratches trouble me deeply, but Milady remains jubilant after such wretched abuse.

"I could never take pleasure in pain," I tell her. "If this is the mark of man, I am safer in my own leanings."

"Ah, but this is no mere man," she says, and closes her eyes. A smile flows from her tender pink lips. "He is a man and so much more."

As Milady skims her fingers through the hair between her legs, I watch her lovely breasts bob in the water. Those pallid spheres call to me, their poor pink nipples distended and erect. I roll up the sleeves of my nightdress before drizzling fragranced oil across her chest. She sighs when I rub my cloth the length of her bare breast, but I am hardly satisfied to touch her skin through a square of cotton. Her nudity provokes irrepressible urges in me. I must feel her soft flesh against mine.

Releasing the cloth, I trace gentle fingertips down her breasts. She whimpers when I fondle her nipples. What that beastly man did to cause her such lasting agony, I'll never know. What can I do but take those floating orbs into the care of my palms and revere them with my soft caress? When I press her breasts together she smiles and sighs. I squeeze them repeatedly, again and again. Slick as they are with lavender oil, they slip one against the other and glide from my hands. I circle the meat of my palms around her beautiful breasts until the bathwater ripples in the tub. If it wasn't for the pain inflicted by that wretched beast, I would plunge my face into her bath and suckle at her bosom until I drowned.

When she returns from him broken and bleeding, what else have I to offer but my gentle hands? Each time she goes to the forest in search of that beast I must remind myself it is my touch she will come home to. I am the woman she sleeps beside each night. No one else but I may caress her soft body underneath the bedcovers. At night, she is mine to embrace. I would never abuse my gift as this horrible man has done time after time. What kind of hideous creature would torture a woman so?

My thighs are slick with juice as I trace my fingers down her stomach. Again I take up my cotton cloth and wipe faint traces of blood from her wounds. Milady whimpers and, opening her eyes, lifts her hand from the bath. When she quaintly pets my cheek with the back of her fingers, I am in heaven.

"Ah, you are a dear," Milady sighs.

Her words tremble inside of me, but I only acknowledge her sentiment with the slightest of nods. I know what I will do next and, though I'm certain she will not put up her guard, my heart pounds inside my chest.

With cloth in hand, I cleanse the length of her thighs. She murmurs her approval each time I approach the abyss. In the illuminated darkness, I can scarcely see her most intimate hair drifting below the water's surface, but I know how to find it. I have touched her there so many times before.

When I set my palm against her mound, she seizes the sides of the tub and gasps. Her wet hair casts water across the floor as she tosses her head side to side against the rim. "My little Lizzie Bet," she coos. "You take such fine care of your mistress, my dear."

I press my lips together until a grin breaks free. In truth, there is nothing I love better than Milady's praise. I rub her mound with the cloth and she writhes beneath my touch.

"All I want is to please you," I confess, though I've told her this before.

Her breath is rough and heavy when she replies, "You do naught *but* to please me, my sweet darling Bet."

With my heart full of joy, I toss away the cotton cloth and kiss her wet flesh with my fingers. The tender place between Milady's thighs is softer than her fine furs or silks, or anything else my hardworking hands have ever touched. Her body is my cathedral, and she my high priestess. I worship at the apex of Milady's tremulous cunt.

Her hips rock the bath in time with my tender strokes. Her pale cheeks flush with exertion as her breath grows rapid and unsteady. As my tempo accelerates, her frenzied motion spills fragranced water over the sides. I rub the lips between her thighs with all my love and might, splashing myself with every stroke. With one hand, I cling to the tub, but the front of my nightdress is already soaked through and my nipples erect with the chill. She stifles the cries I've so often heard stifled. We know we must be quiet. In this house, the walls have ears.

When her bliss has ebbed and flowed, I stroke her mound slowly. She mumbles my name in all its forms, calling me Lizzie, Betty, Beth and Bet, and spouting tender messages of adoration. My heart is never so full as when Milady speaks my name. Her loving compliments are my absinthe. I massage her most tender flesh until the bath turns cold and my wet nightdress chills me to the bone. Then, I wrap her hair in fine linens and cloak her wounded body in fresh silks. For this one night, I will sleep nude.

Milady's breath grows deep the moment we crawl into bed, but my relief at her safe return overshadows my desire to whisper words of love. I envelop her tender form in my arms. Even in sleep, she flinches at my touch. When I close my eyes, I see the horrific vision of her backside trickling with semen and blood. I shudder and hold her body closer to mine. Seeing her secretive grin in my mind's eye, I wonder what inspired it.

The full moon shines bright outside Milady's window. A lone wolf howls in the distance. Despite my exhaustion, I cannot sleep. What creature would do such harm to a lovely young woman? And to what end does Milady seek the damage?

THE WAY HOME

Carrie Williams

She had meant to ride all day and into the night, catching the dawn ferry and getting back by noon. But about halfway between the Med and the Channel, on a deserted rural road somewhere between Roanne and Nevers, she had seen the amber light spilling out onto the water and decided to stop for a *steak-frites* and some beer, figuring that this might be the last place she'd see open for food before morning.

Riding up to the back of the squat rectangular building, past the parking area and a little children's playground, she cut her engine and walked around to the lakeside entrance. Through a glass door she could see two men still in blue work overalls gazing at a screen in the corner. As she pulled it open and stepped in, they turned to look at her, though their gazes remained curiously blank, and they turned back to their glasses of red wine without making any form of greeting.

She approached the bar, pulled back one of the stools and hoisted herself onto it, placing her helmet on the flat surface of the *zinc*. The man behind it was watching the match too, mechanically polishing a glass with a cloth. He seemed unaware of her presence, and she had to clear her throat to draw his attention. He turned to her, eyebrows slightly raised. He had black tousled hair, an unmemorable face.

"*Un bière*," she said, reaching into the pocket of her leather jacket for her matches and lighting a cigarette.

The man turned away for a glass, drew some pale-gold liquid into it and passed it over to her with a fresh beer-mat.

"*Merci*," she said, but he had already turned back to the screen and seemed not to hear her.

She sat and smoked; drank another beer, then a third; decided she wasn't hungry after all. She watched as the workmen stood up and took leave of the barman with a brief wave, then she fumbled in her pockets for some notes. As she did so, another glass, beaded with condensation, materialized in front of her. She looked up.

"*Cadeau*," said the barman. "On the house."

She smiled and raised the glass to him. He was watching her, unsmiling. Her stomach flipped over. Marc was only eight hours behind her and yet already a lifetime away. Who knew, anyway, if she'd ever see him again? It seemed unlikely, after the way they'd parted. She shifted on her stool, looked away and then back. This time she held the stare.

She lit a cigarette in the darkness and glanced at the black mass beside her. She didn't think he was sleeping, but he certainly didn't want to make any polite chat. She knew only that his name was Freddy and that this was his bar. What more did she need to know?

Not sleepy at all, she wondered if she should pick up her clothes from around the bed, dress and ride out again into the night. Tunbridge Wells, and a warm bath, beckoned across the miles, across the sea. Yet here was a bed, shelter until morning. What was the hurry after all?

She got up and slipped on her knickers and bra, pulling his T-shirt over them for want of being able to find her sweatshirt. It reached almost to her knees and smelled of cigarette smoke and cooking oil and sweat. She opened the door and stepped through into the bar, where her empty glass and full ashtray still rested on the counter. He had thought to turn the lights and the TV off, but the moon beyond the French windows bathed the room in its white glow. She took her cigarettes, cracked the lock on the door and stepped out onto the terrace.

It was some kind of artificial lake, perhaps in an old quarry. On either side of the terrace jutting out over the shore, small beaches had been created of fine sand dotted with occasional pebbles and shells and larger rocks. To her left she could just make out the sign for a campsite that must have been hidden by the line of trees; to her right was the playground. The terrace itself was laid with metal tables and chairs for warmer evenings. She pulled back one of the chairs and sat down.

The water stretched out before her, placidly reflecting the moonlight. She extended her legs and gazed down at the lake as she exhaled smoke into the cool night air. Only twelve hours previously she had been on the beach at Cannes. She could almost feel the water on her bronzed skin, smell the salt. It made her want to strip off Freddy's T-shirt and step down onto the narrow strip of sand and into the water. It would be cold, surely, but refreshing after the long ride and the sex.

But then she thought she could maybe sleep after all; she should at least try if she wanted to get an early start on the road.

* * *

Grinding a cigarette into the ashtray, she stood up from the bar and made her way to the kitchen. She picked up the small square of paper, frowned to decipher Freddy's squiggle, then turned and lit two of the gas burners. Placing a pan on each, she threw a forkful of butter into both of them and listened for their sizzle as she bent to take two raw steaks from the fridge.

She had never worked as a chef, but from odd jobs here and there she was competent enough with the basics—omelettes, grills, oysters, salads, *mousse au chocolat*—to take over in the kitchen when Freddy suggested it. She'd taken that as his way of asking her to stay and accepted the proposal without hesitation. She'd even told him she would think about selling the bike and use the money to smarten the place up a little, give it a lick of paint and expand the menu.

And so she found herself in the kitchen, twice a day. Lunchtimes were hardest, with local workers and lorry drivers coming in to refuel; evenings were much quieter. She was generally through by nine, when she would hang up her apron and shake down her hair then wander through and sit and smoke at the bar, watching him pour wine, wipe glasses, stare up at the football. Then they'd lock the door and turn out the lights and go out back, to his small, bare bedroom, and fuck, wordlessly, until sleep at last took hold.

She still didn't know what kept her back, that first morning. She knew only that she'd woken alone, still wearing Freddy's T-shirt, and walked out onto the terrace where he sat on the same chair she'd occupied in the early hours of the morning. He was clad only in his boxers, and he was running his fingers through his sleep-mussed hair as he stared out over the glittering water. There was something about his face, an emptiness that pinched at her heart. She stepped up behind him, placed her arms around his shoulders and thought she'd maybe stay for another day.

That was three weeks ago now, but it could have been years. Already they were like an old married couple, set in their routines. She was surprised to find how comforting that could be, after ten years of moving around, thinking that that was the only way of really being alive. Or was this not a life? Was the sex—mute but full of a kind of furious energy—blinding her to that?

Except on Sundays, when the restaurant and bar were closed and they stayed in bed all day, they rose around ten and, after a cigarette and an espresso on the terrace, she went to prepare things in the kitchen—peel potatoes, wash lettuce, chop onions—and he got the bar ready, drove to the bakery for baguettes, emptied the bins and did anything else that needed attending to. The day took its course. At about two thirty, after the lunchtime rush, things would slacken off for her, and she would go and take a siesta or, if it was warm, bring a book out onto the terrace and sit blinking in the sunshine, the changing light on the water sending her into a sort of trance. She never opened her book. There was something so seductive about not thinking at all. She felt she had switched her brain off and was living entirely through her cunt. There was a lot to be said for that. It made life remarkably uncomplicated. She had had far too much of complicated.

It was the end of that third week when she woke and went to pee and saw, in the mirror above the sink, the mark on her throat. She thought at first of Freddy, of the almost desperate savagery of his lovemaking. Bearing down on her, large hands firm on her frail shoulders, he'd drive into her with a kind of fury, saying nothing. She'd try to push him up and away from her, so that she could see his face, look into his eyes, somehow read him, but he'd crush his face against her shoulder, and as she began to shudder toward her climax, she'd feel his mouth open and close against her skin, as if he were trying to say something to her after all. His orgasm, immediately following and indeed unleashed by hers, would resemble a falling away, as if Freddy had stepped backward off a cliff and into the abyss.

But continuing to stare enthralled at her reflection, she knew that this wasn't the evidence of a mouth, the over-enthusiastic nip of a lover's teeth. This was a hand, nails. She wondered if, in the throes of her last climax, she might have clawed at herself, but she told herself she would surely have been aware that she had torn open her own flesh.

No, it just wasn't possible. And yet how had this wound come about without her knowledge? She brought her fingers to it and winced. How could she not have screamed out in pain when it happened, not have even noticed? She shook her head, pulled open the bathroom cabinet and delved inside, trying to find some kind of antiseptic, a box of plasters.

Back in bed, the wound sealed, she stared at the ceiling, then at Freddy's back. What did she know of this man, after all? He spoke so little. She didn't know where he had come from, where he was going, the root of the void she saw in his eyes. That was what had attracted her: she was sick of hearing about people's pasts, how they had fucked up their lives. Perhaps, she thought now, he was silent because he had something to hide.

She dressed in the dark, walked out onto the terrace and then around to the back of the building, and looked at her bike. There it was, covered in tarpaulin, ready for her to make her escape. What was she waiting for? She reached out and touched it. She needed only her backpack and helmet, and she could be away into the night. Freddy would wake up and shrug and in a few hours it would seem like it had all been a dream, for both of them: nebulous, unformed as an embryo.

She walked back around to the terrace and sat down. The water slurped at the shore, whipped up by a northerly wind. She stood up and looked down into it. She hadn't even swum here yet. She pulled off her top, slipped her jeans down and shucked them off her ankles, then stepped down onto the strip of beach to her left and walked slowly into the water. It was cold on her ankles, on her thighs, on her cunt, but she carried on in, until she was waist deep, surrounded by the inky substance. Her arms were crossed over her chest, one hand on each shoulder. She closed her eyes and advanced.

She opened them with a start, as if coming to, as if returning from another place. The water was just below her mouth, and if she carried on any farther she would be submerged. The plaster on her neck was coming loose, and she worried that the wound would become infected by something in the water. She turned around and waded out. It seemed to take forever, where walking in had taken mere seconds. She ran up onto the terrace, grabbed her clothes and hurried inside the bar.

Freddy was still asleep, curled up fetally on his half of the bed. Since there was no window—his room must back onto the little slip road leading to the campsite—she was only able to see him because he left the bathroom light on for security. There had been two attempted break-ins, he had told her, in the last year.

She sat on the bed; laid one hand on his broad, muscular back and enjoyed his animal heat after the shock of the cold water. He stirred, moaned something that she couldn't match up with any word she knew. She climbed up onto him, causing him to roll onto his back, took his prick in her hand and worked at him until his eyes half opened in recognition, then she mounted him. Assertive in bed with every man she'd been with until now, she had found herself curiously submissive with Freddy since this affair began. And he had hardly encouraged her to be adventurous, pushing her down onto his mattress with the heel of one hand, spreading her legs with one deft, almost perfunctory movement. She'd quite liked that at first, the feeling that he was mastering her, brooking no dissent on her part. There was the feeling that he was *taking* her, almost against her will, and she had enjoyed that more than she would have expected to.

But now it was time to shake things up, to summon up her own pleasure and not let it be something inflicted on her by some external force. Freddy's eyes were closed tight again, as if against a fierce light. Unable to burrow his face into her shoulder, this was his only recourse, other than blindfolding himself with his hands. These lay curiously lifeless beside him as she now rode him, she noticed. Sighing, she reached down between her legs and prized her lips apart where they folded around his cock. Then with one finger she flicked at her clitoris and teased herself into greater excitement.

Involuntarily, Freddy's hand rose in a spasm, touching the bandage on her neck. She felt his hand linger, the barest moment, but he didn't open his eyes, nor did he ask any questions—he merely grazed the fabric with his fingertips and then brought his hands down to her hips, securing her to him as she came.

Afterward she told him a little about herself. Not because she thought it mattered to him—who she was, who she had been—but to fill the silence. When she finished speaking, knowing that he had slept through most of her words, she lay still, listening, above the regular tide of his breathing, for the sound of the lake as it met the shore, chided by the wind. Its presence there, through the half-open door and beyond the French windows of the bar, was somehow comforting. For a moment it almost seemed to beckon her: a second lover. But when she rose, obeying its call, and stood looking out over it from the terrace, she was frightened by the cold hard sheen of its surface, making it appear almost solid, and hurried back inside, thinking of Freddy's eyes. She switched on the TV, turned off the sound, and sat in the flickering light it cast, resisting the pull of both the lake and the spartan room where Freddy slept.

He left the next day, on an overnight trip to visit his mother in Bourges. She was ailing, he told her; she knew he didn't want her to ask more.

He was replaced at the bar by Georges, who came to drink there perhaps once a week, remaining largely silent. That wasn't unusual, but she often felt, when she crossed the bar carrying plates laden with food, that he was observing Freddy as the latter gazed at the TV, that he was interrogating him with his eyes. He seemed an odd choice for a replacement, even for a single night. But Freddy had told her that Georges worked in a bar in nearby Moulins, that he had lots of experience and that he trusted him.

The bar was quiet anyway, almost deserted that night. They may as well not have opened. Not long past nine, Georges opened the door to the kitchen, where she was reading a newspaper, and told her that the last customer had left. He was famished, he said; why didn't she cook them up a steak before he headed off? Nice and rare.

She hadn't eaten since lunchtime, and the prospect of a good thick steak was alluring. As he disappeared back into the bar, she sought one out in the fridge and lit the burners. Taking the sharpest knife from the rack, she placed the tip on one edge of the meat and drew it back, to slice it in half. The flesh gave beneath the blade as if she was discovering an old wound.

She felt hands on her shoulders; she hadn't heard the door

reopen behind her, she'd been so intent on her task, so mesmerized by the sticky, hot-red leak of the meat. She stiffened. The
hand moved down, over her thin ribs, her hips, hooked themselves around her. She held her breath.

"Looks good," came Georges's voice at her ear.

"Please," she moaned. "Don't..." Her grasp tightened on the
knife, then grew slack as she felt herself yield. What harm would
it do, she said to herself, to submit? Georges was a good-looking
man, and she felt it was unlikely that he would tell Freddy. And
Freddy—what was he to her anyway? There could have been
something there, if he had opened up to her. But looking into his
empty eyes, as they fucked, was like falling into a black hole.

His fingers were inside her pants now, prizing her apart,
tracing the wet slit of her, purplish and frilled. She eased the
knifepoint a little farther along the meat, felt her grip tautening
again.

"Please, no," she said. "Just—just go now. Before it's too
late."

His teeth were on her shoulder, biting, coaxing. "C'mon,"
she heard him say. "What have you got to lose? Everyone knows
Freddy can't make a woman happy."

She spun around, and the knife flashed dangerously between
them, close to his throat.

"What do you mean?" she hissed, eyes narrowed.

Georges had stepped back, arms up as if in surrender. Then
he turned toward the door back to the bar. "Just ask him," he
said as he walked out, already reaching for his jacket on the
end of the bar, "where his wife and daughter are now. Ask him
that."

She placed the knife beside the oozing meat, fumbled for the
cigarettes in her apron pocket, and stood smoking as she listened
to Georges's motorbike start up with a roar. Attentive to its

dwindling as he turned onto the main road and then vanished in the direction of Moulins, she turned off all the lights and went to bed.

Things continued as normal on Freddy's return, whatever "normal" could mean in a place like this, with a man like this. She didn't—couldn't—ask him about his wife and child, for fear of unpicking scars that might still be unhealed—but also because they talked of nothing at all. Sometimes the question formed itself in her throat, and she could taste the words in her mouth, slightly metallic, as if they'd bubbled up inside her, in spite of herself. But when she opened her mouth, nothing came out. The silence between them had congealed, set, become something tangible. It was the only thing that was real.

She went to sit on her bike, under its tarp, and tried to imagine the thrum of it between her legs, its power as it surged forward across tarmac, carrying her into a future she didn't yet know. But where that uncertainty had used to thrill her, now it made her afraid. More afraid than staying here with this man she would never know, this man who had somehow lost his family, through carelessness or design she didn't know. Something inside her had changed; a fire had gone out. Where before she could never stay still, now she seemed unable to move.

She'd often step out of the kitchen and study Freddy as he polished the glasses and stared unseeing at the TV screen. She wondered if she should fear him, if the absence she felt in him was an absence of remorse. But even as they closed up for yet another night and she gave herself to him, as she gave herself to him every night, without hesitation or any holding back, there was something inside that knew that he hadn't killed them, that he wasn't a killer. That she was safe in his hands if not secure in his heart.

* * *

A month and a half, two months—she'd kept no note of time. She might even have said it had started to feel like home, if she knew what "home" meant, what it was to have one. There was another slash on her neck, from halfway up the right side of it to her clavicle, swooping around. She stood in front of the mirror, tracing it with her fingers. Freddy said nothing. It looked like the trajectory of a fingernail, a sharp fingernail. She covered it up well before her swim, which had become daily now, despite the cooling of the days as summer ceded to autumn.

Custom fell off, especially in the evenings. It struck her that no children ever came to the playground or the beach, even in summer. On a rare trip into the village to buy bread one day when Freddy had to go to the wholesaler, she found herself asking the *boulanger*'s wife about it. She hadn't planned to, and she did so more, it struck her later, to draw out the conversation than because the question had been plaguing her.

The woman shrugged, seemed to avoid her gaze now. "*Mais depuis l'accident...*"

"*L'accident?*"

"*Oui...accident...ou bien...*" Her words tailed off; she seemed to be transfixed by something beyond the window, in the empty street.

So there was an accident, or something like it. He didn't kill them—her trust was vindicated. You don't fuck a murderer and not feel it.

She walked home, kicking at fallen leaves. Yes, this was her home now. She would never leave. Something tied her to the place, if not to Freddy—something that hadn't tied her to Cannes, to Ventimiglia, to Palermo, to any of the places she had been. She told herself that she would probably never know what it was; that it didn't, in the end, matter.

Sex, that night, was like a slow engulfing, an obliteration. This time she made no effort to assert herself or her needs, but instead lay solemnly back on the stained sheets, hair fanned out around her, and let Freddy thrust and thrust, unceasingly, as she came over and over, each orgasm seeming to call forth another, until she began to fear she would never be sated and must eventually lose her mind. She wondered that he could hold out so long—normally when she came, her contractions would set him off and he'd erupt inside her with an animalistic cry, half ecstasy, half pain. This time was different. This time it seemed as if his body and not only his mind was beyond reach, and finally he simply rolled off her and went to sleep without comment.

Afterward, she took her cigarettes and went to sit on the terrace. The water stirred only lightly in the breeze, like a chest rising and falling gently in the deepest of sleeps. She stripped, finished her cigarette and waded in, taking care over the sharp little stones of the foreshore. Farther in, a patch of weeds crisscrossed around her ankles, gluey, jelly-like, thicker and more tenacious than one might have expected. She marched on, freeing herself, toward the middle of the lake, where she knew it was clearer, purer.

The water rose up her naked flesh, wrapped itself around her like an icy shroud. Normally sensitive to the cold, an aficionado of warm climes, she welcomed its chill, carried on even beyond the point where she feared going under completely. Just before her mouth and then her nose were covered, she inhaled instinctively, although she knew she wouldn't be coming back up. But she wanted to feel, for as long as possible, the tiny hands on her ankles, the larger ones at her throat, holding her in a grip that seemed like a caress, prying at her flesh, pulling her down. Letting her know where home really was, where happiness truly lay.

THE QUEEN

Tahira Iqbal

It's something else, being with him. I've never felt safer: our colliding bodies, our fitting frame. He chants dangerous words into my ear, words that threaten my undoing as his hand travels slowly up my stomach until he cups the lower swell of my breast. He's dark. The steel shadows that he offers me instead of a wide, easy smile always allude to darkness.

"Amelia..." he breathes, sliding into me. "Still... Still yourself..."

I bite down on my lip, trying not to shake under his weight. His hand goes fully around my breast. He presses searching lips against the violent pulse in my neck, a pulse that only he can send into flight. His teeth are sharp and he sends the fine points sliding into my skin.

Here comes the calm, the utter serenity that only he can bring. He lifts the charge out of my system with easy draws, leaving me limp under him and listening to his soft moans of pleasure as he tastes the high that's running my system. His bare chest rises, flaring, enjoying the power that he always has over me. His throaty laugh is one of victory when I moan his name as his teeth extract.

He trails hot, wet kisses down my bare chest, his lips leaving bloody prints in a zigzag pattern down my torso. I weave fingers into his dark hair, enjoying the descent...that's about to go supersonic. His lips...tongue...search... And find.

My spine arches, sending a beautiful torture through me that ends with a sigh of utter satiation as he bites. Hard. Teeth sink into my inner thigh and fingers go in, to settle, to stir the wetness. He feeds on my senses, burning me up with the fierce prowess that he owns.

"You want me..." He licks my inner thigh, collecting blood, wet heat.

"I want you," I whisper. "Always."

He rises, showing me stained lips that he licks with slow delight. His brilliant emerald eyes flash with color. His erect cock bumps my stomach.

"Take me," he says. I grasp his cock, barely able to make a fist around it as I guide him in, ensuring a tight fit. He rests just the tip inside, the bold threat of promise.... Dazzling. I shiver under his possession as his eyes light up. Then he's inside of me with one swift stroke, one breathy moan. My gasp leaves my chest in a rush.

"Come for me, Amelia," he says, and thrusts. It's not slow. It's not measured. He's taking me hard. Fast. The pressure is thunderous. Blood heats. Everything inside melts. I get his mouth on mine, tasting myself. I reach around, hands on his muscular back, desperate to keep the connection there for as long as I can. He drives the passion with brute finesse, allowing me to rise into the charge, brimming with static.

"Come." His voice is nothing more than an unearthly rumble

as his animal side vaults into being. I bang headlong into a fit of pure delight that steals all breath, all focus. He's still hard, intent on prolonging his desire.

"Hours Amelia…" the King whispers. "We've got hours…" And he kisses me. It's not delicate. It's not tender. It's to claim me. Like he's done for hundreds of years. And as always, I love it.

I rise alone. The large bed that I've shared with the King is nothing but twisted, blood-stained sheets. I take a shower; change into denims, shirt and jumper; wind my long raven-colored hair into a knot. It's barely midnight. He doesn't always stay the night, but he sticks to his promises. Hours. I always get hours.

I leave my bedroom, trekking down the dark corridor. Our house is large, built hundreds of years ago by the King to his exacting specifications. Dark room after dark room filled with celebrated furniture that would fetch millions if it ever went to auction. The estate is secluded but rambling, extending for lush long miles.

I stop at Marial's room and put a palm up against the stained wood. She's not there. I head toward Katya's room and feel the door. Barbs of heat circle my palm, stinging me like a viper. I get rough tingles through my body ending between my legs. She's there. With Marial and the King.

I head downstairs, passing the guards at the front door with a nod. The threat of assassination is always present and the King takes no chances with our safety. I head to the kitchen, pick a vial of blood from the fridge. I down it standing at the window, tracing snowflakes as they drift from a black sky, twinkling as they get picked out by the floodlights.

"I'm going for a walk," I say to the guards, as I reach for my coat and replace my trainers with boots. The estate is protected by a sophisticated security system as well as a team of men that patrol the acres with guns at their sides. I'll be followed, but I always ask them to keep their distance.

Moonlight helps me pick out a path, although my eyes are wide, easily absorbing the dark, converting it into perfect vision. The land is quiet except for the hush of deer hooves against fresh snow, wings against foliage. I reach the frozen lake, taking a seat on the bench after wiping away the inches of snow.

I've been with the King for nearly three hundred years. He'd taken my virginity and life on one hot Parisian summer night at his family's estate. I'd taken the invite with blushing cheer when he visited the boarding house my parents ran, inviting townsfolk to a party. At seventeen I'd gone doe-eyed for the handsome rich man from the next village. Such sweetness had fallen from his lips, such elegance and sureness, that I skipped dinner, feigning that I felt unwell. My parents had declined the offer, but I'd tucked my pillows under my bedclothes and crept out of the house using the staff entrance.

The party had been in full swing by the time I had reached the estate. Dressed in my finest, my hair loose and down to my waist, I'd tossed off the long hooded cloak, leaving it with a housemaid, and eagerly swept into the big, candlelit house, filled with elegantly dressed people. With awfully, awfully sharp teeth.

"Amelia."

I'm startled by the King's presence so deep has been my reverie. He's not alone. A bodyguard stands a few meters away. Landon Barnes I think his name is. He carries a torch, but doesn't look in my direction; he never does. His eyes are always trained on whatever he perceives as potential danger. The newest recruit to the security team, the ex-soldier doesn't say much, but he makes up for it with his sheer physical presence. He's got a body that could take down angry men or bright-eyed women.

And his scent... It drugs the deepest veins I have. He doesn't talk about his life, but in his storm-gray eyes, sometimes I catch a haunted thought, which he always blinks away, leaving a focused duty. And he's unafraid of vampires.

"My King," I say as my lover takes a seat beside me, his arm going around the back of the bench. He's dressed in dark clothes, heavy boots on his feet.

"You're far away," he says.

"I was thinking about Paris."

He laughs with remembrance. Three. He always has three women in his court... And that night, I joined the ranks after the death of my predecessor some months previously. Strikingly blonde and both beautiful, Marial and Katya have been by his side for nearly a thousand years, making them nearly as old as the King.

Both of us stare out along the dark and icy water. There's a fox on the other side of the lake picking at the ground. It senses our rough, strange presences. It doesn't like them and dashes off. I tip my head up, letting the flakes rest on my face.

"Why me?"

"It was your sharp eyes and sharp senses. I knew it the moment I saw you, beautiful one."

I'd rested against his chest for hours after, Marial and Katya naked at the foot of the bed, watching me change with rapt fascination. I shiver, recalling how the door had been kicked in the moment I'd changed. I'd been dragged off the linens, and into the vise-like hands of...

"Don't think about him," the King warns softly, lips kissing my temple. "I would never let anyone hurt you. Any of you."

"Your brother is dangerous," I say. "I know that you've increased the security personnel."

"The Sovereign will not get what he wants. There's an order.

And he's not part of it." He looks up at the starry sky. "I've already chosen my successor."

"My King..." I gasp. "No... That's like accepting defeat!"

He takes my hand, kisses the back of it.

"No. It's merely a precaution. I plan to be around for eras and eons."

My choked sob delivers him closer. He wraps me up against him.

"Most women would be pleased to know that they are going to be the Queen. Ruler of our kind."

My open-mouthed stare makes him smile.

"But Marial, Katya... They've been with you for longer!" I stammer.

"You know that time is irrelevant to us! Besides, I've already informed the Elders."

"My King..."

"I was in Geneva last week for business, so I arranged a meeting." His eyes flash with heat. "Now. Let's go back to bed." He helps me to my feet, walking me back to the house, the silent bodyguard leading the way.

In the morning, I change carefully. The King is sprawled out beside me, nude in tangled sheets. I've got bruises on my hips from where he took me fiercely up against the tiles in the en suite shower.

By the time I head downstairs, the ache is gone. Light streams through the stained-glass windows flanking the huge wooden front door.

"I'm going into the village," I say to the day-shift guards. One of them reaches for his walkie-talkie.

There's some focused talk and one minute later, Landon arrives. He's wearing black trousers and a gray jumper that makes his eyes opaque. He reaches for his parka and we exit the house together, heading toward a 4 x 4.

The sun breaks through the clouds, showering the acreage with beauty, igniting the thick layers of snow. Landon slips on aviator-style sunglasses as we drive through the large gates.

Thirty minutes later, I meet our blood contact and exchange a thick collection of notes. Landon helps me put the vials of blood into the hatch of the 4 x 4. I'm about to get into the car when sensational pressure knocks out my knees. My moan of shock draws Landon to my side, a weapon already in his hands. He helps me upright, allowing me to rest against his solid frame.

"Landon..." His dark eyes mesh with mine. "Something's happened at the house!"

The 4 x 4 lurches. The gate barely swings open as he fires the car up the driveway. It's a good few minutes before we see the imposing house. He won't let me out to run, to get to the house in seconds, rather than minutes.

The car skids to a halt. Landon reaches inside of his parka, draws his gun.

"Stay here, the car's bulletproof." He checks the chamber, sure that he's got enough wooden bullets.

"You're not," I breathe as he pops the glove compartment, extracts a clip and puts it into his pocket. A hunger comes over his eyes that startles me with its ferocity.

I watch him disappear into the house. The front door is wide open. There's blood on the doorstep, patches of it on the snow. I search the arched windows, eyes trekking floor to floor, window to window. But there's no movement. I can't sense anything. I put my palm up against the glass but I'm too far away. All I can feel is the heat of the sun.

"Shit!" I need to get to the house. If I can just palm the masonry it'll tell me all that I need to know. I open the door and run, crossing meters in milliseconds. My hand goes flat against the wall.

I wrench it away. *No! Marial...Katya... Oh no!* I run inside, skidding on the blood of the guards, their dismembered bodies strewn about the lofty reception hall.

"Amelia!" I hear Landon's voice, trace his fast descending figure down the stairs. "We have to go! Now!" I'm grabbed by Landon, thrust toward the front door.

I slap my palm against the wood, take one last toke of the ether... My scream of horror sends a crack into the foundations. The King...he's dead.

I'm taken to an apartment in the city. I get shown into a living room; large windows run floor to ceiling, showing me a striking outline of a river and the buildings that sweep down its curving path.

"Here, drink this." Landon takes out a small golden vial from his breast pocket. I take it, suddenly aware that my hands are shaking. I hadn't noticed the tremor, and I'm touched that he did. I down the liquid, heating instantly, the shock abating so that I can focus.

"You were there at the lake. You heard what the King said..." My chest aches from the loss of my family as I take a seat on a couch. "I can't believe this is happening."

Landon pulls out his phone, speed dials a number. Clearly he doesn't want me to hear the conversation, because he leaves the room. Which is stupid... I rise, heading to the glass windows to press a palm against the pane and listen.

He's talking to someone, sharing the event with distinct detail. His voice is even, never betraying the panic of the situation. His rapid and clearly well thought out battle plan is rapped out to someone he clearly trusts.

I lower my palm. There's a push in my gut as tears roll free.

"Amelia," Landon says, coming back into the room. "Don't stand near the windows."

No sooner have the words left his mouth than there's a small sound of glass cracking. The bullet comes through the pane with frightening speed and goes thumping into my shoulder.

I get tossed back with the force; the lightning-sharp pain ensures that I'm pinned to the floor, screams caught in my throat. Landon drags me up against his side, running with me as a hail of bullets spears the room. I pant in delirium, the wound sizzling as we run to the 4 x 4 in the underground garage.

"Landon...get it out...it's oak." My hands shake far too violently to even attempt an extraction, but Landon doesn't hesitate as he puts me on the back seat of the 4 x 4. He straddles me, ripping my shirt, exposing the bloody shoulder. He pulls a knife from a sheath attached to his calf. He meets my gaze; his eyes go hard. He stabs in, cutting swiftly around the wound.

I bear down, aware that my fangs are descending, basic inner senses perceiving this as an attack. Hands go into fists as I break apart under him. My unearthly scream gets no attention from him. The wound pops and Landon's fingers grab the bullet. He tosses it out the door.

He drives as I dig in the hatch, grabbing a blood vial. I down half of it and tip the rest over my wound. I sink on the backseat, aware that the world is spinning, and that I'm unable to respond to Landon's concerned calls as darkness claims my vision.

I awaken on a sofa. Landon's at the fireplace, standing sentry, watching the flames twist and move. My shoulder no longer vibrates with pain, but I'm covered in dried blood. My shirt hangs open, my bra visible.

"Where's the bathroom?" I say hoarsely as I sit up. My throat is sore as if I've been screaming.

"Upstairs," he says without looking at me.

"You don't know what you're asking..." I breathe against his scented neck.

"If it means I get to be with you forever..." His hand roves up my back, caressing softly, "then I'm taking that deal."

Those words reach into my senses.

"I thought you didn't like me? You're always so stand-offish..."

He weaves careful fingers into my hair.

"Didn't like you? Hell, I wanted you from the moment I saw you..." His lips come down to mine; this time the exploration is tender, designed to steal breath.

He takes me by the hand, leading me upstairs where he lights a few candles.

I take a seat on a large bed. He strips my shirt, my bra off with eager, steady, exploring hands. His fingers sweep the site of the bullet wound again, a soft laugh leaving his lips as he finds that there's really nothing there. He kneels, eyes alight with passion, sending a roaring thrill through me.

"You're sure?" I breathe as his mouth finds a nipple. He sucks. Hard. I shiver under the touch. He rises, pressing kisses into my hairline before shoving off his shirt. He's got striking tribal-style tattoos marking the expanse of his chest, but among them sit scars; some barely there, others deep enough to distort his flesh. I lean in, kissing a healed tear. His moan of pleasure comes hurtling from the depths of his chest.

"I need to feel you..." he says huskily.

I lie back, watching as he leans in, undoing the button, then the zipper of my denims, taking them off, tossing them to the floor. He strips, his erection boldly jutting out from his body. He tugs my panties off then leans down, his mouth kissing a hot trail from knee to upper thigh. He presses his tongue against my clit, sending me roaring into the heavens. I fist his hair, keen to keep him there, but aching, desperately aching for more.

He gets the hint and lifts, kissing me, letting me taste myself. And then he's inside of me. One swift thrust, a sure connection. His body rises majestically over me, and the scent of his warming, soaring blood sends me flying. I look up into those glorious eyes, naked desire beating a hard rhythm.

I place a hand at the back of his neck to draw him down. He thinks I'm going to kiss him. He stiffens with a tiny sliver of panic as he sees my fangs. But this man has fought in wars, faced many marching terrors, even the Sovereign. He blinks. And then there's nothing but determination.

I sink my teeth into his jugular vein. It's the merest slicing of flesh that leaks a heady river of warmth onto my lips. I drink, slowly, softly, ensuring that he's not affected by the drain just yet. Landon grunts with effort as his thrusts deepen, strengthen. I inhale his scent, drag more of him into my mouth. I wrap my legs around his waist, drawing him impossibly deeper. I stop drinking and slide the venom down my fangs into his blood.

"I'm coming..." Landon moans softly. I drag my teeth down his neck, ripping open serious inches of flesh. The writhing man above me comes deep inside and loses power in the next second.

Rolling him onto his back, staying connected with him, enjoying the spiral of my own orgasm, I concentrate on the fierceness of the fight in his eyes. Duty. It's all about duty. I wrap my palm around his exposed throat. He bites down.

"Don't fight it..." I whisper, staying as still as I can, his cock pressing up against the mouth of my womb, splinters of wonderful delight bumping every nerve as I come.

He pants now, his color lowering wildly as he rides an epic wave of sensation that sends a furious vibration through his body. I draw away my hand to see that the wound is still bleeding violently, the sheets under him stained. He tries to sit up, but I plant a firm hand on his chest, watching as his eyes go still.

Minutes tick by. I stay there, connected, ensuring that the venom is circulating.

His gasp into waking nearly knocks me off the bed. His fists fly at the dangerous shadows he perceives... I comfort him as he groans, twisting his neck, feeling the rapid cramping that signifies healing. He palms the closed flesh, mesmerized by the lack of stain. His gaze connects with mine. Gone is that storm gray. Emerald. He's got emerald eyes like mine.

"Ready to fight that war?" I say. Landon looks down, new eyes taking in the blood on my lips, the trail of it down my chin, my breasts, the intimate connection that we're still keeping. He flips me onto my back, his ethereal speed sending a coarse charge through me.

"Ready," says a dark new voice that vibrates with promise.

BENEDICTION

Bonnie Dee

He must have been asleep when they brought in his new cell-mate, although how he hadn't noticed the noise of the door opening or shutting was a mystery. For that matter, he couldn't really recall waking. Since night and day were interchangeable here, he didn't call his occasional lapses of consciousness true sleep, merely a lull in the monotony of eternal night.

Suddenly another person was simply there with him in the darkness. His solitary confinement was evidently over. Maybe even here in Hell they'd run out of space after eons and had to double up their prisoners. He laughed at the irony of shared solitary, a dry sound like a broom sweeping a floor. He hadn't meant to laugh aloud. The newcomer would think he was crazy.

As Micah stared at the figure, which definitely seemed to be feminine, his eyes began to burn and he could no longer bear to look at her. *Too bright.* How was that possible? There was no light in this place, never had been, and yet the being standing near the door was clearly illuminated. Had she sifted in through the cracks like snow and filled the chamber with her light? Every detail of her form was etched on his retinas even after he looked away. She was flame fashioned into the white-hot shape of an exquisite woman. But her sheer perfection told him she was not mortal. She merely wore the garb of a body for the present.

"What are you doing here?" His voice cracked, his throat so parched and lips so dry that they threatened to crumble away like a sun-baked sandcastle.

"I'm here for you, Micah." Her voice was cool water filling in the cracks and fissures of his droughty soul. "Are you ready to be free?"

It was a trick. She'd been sent to fool him, to tease him with promises and entice him with her beauty before the door was slammed closed, locking him into this nightmare for another age. She was a new form of torture. He mustn't fall for it.

"Fuck off," he growled, stalking to the opposite wall, only a few paces away.

Her voice flowed around him, as seductive as a smile, sweeter than a kiss. "Think, Micah. Why would someone like me be cast down here? You know what I am."

He risked a glance at her and his stomach hurtled through space at the glorious vision. "And you know what *I* am," he replied. "Why in God's name would you help me get out of here?"

She laughed and the joyful sound seized him and nearly shook him apart. "In God's name, indeed." She moved through the darkness toward him.

He flattened against the wall, terrified of her touch, and winced as she reached out a hand to stroke the side of his face. But her caress didn't burn. Instead smooth satin stroked his cheek. Micah closed his eyes, clenching his jaw tight, waiting for the agony to be over. His eyes ached. His chest hurt. He longed for darkness and solitude once more.

"Don't," he whispered and at last she removed her hand from his face. He drew a deep breath of the sulfurous air of his cell and felt better.

"Haven't you suffered long enough?" Her gentle tone pried his eyes open.

He gazed into her shifting kaleidoscope face. "It's not up to me."

"Of course it is. It always has been. You continue to punish yourself for your sins. But some feel it's past time you let yourself go free."

"Who?"

"Me, for one."

"And who are you?"

"You may call me Hasdiel. I offer you peace and comfort—if you're brave enough to accept those gifts."

Micah really wasn't up to figuring out her riddles and whether she was the angel she represented herself to be or another agent of his destruction. He was too tired and just wanted to be left alone. Loneliness was at least familiar.

"You can trust me," she assured him as if reading his thoughts. "Do you honestly believe the dark forces could create me simply to torment you?"

He looked at her crystalline form—pure energy, pure light—and shook his head. "No. But I still don't understand what you want with me."

"I told you. It's time for you to let go of your past and come into the light. I'm here to guide you. I can't be much clearer than that." She smiled and his heart pounded in his chest as it hadn't in over a thousand years.

Micah swallowed. Parts of his body that had stopped

working long ago began to grind back to life. Since he'd been locked in this prison of the mind for so long, his body a mere bit of extraneous garb, he'd nearly forgotten the things his physical form could do, how it could react with joy and excitement to the presence of another being. Hasdiel took his hand and blood coursed through him and his cells tingled.

"Come, sit with me."

He walked with her across the cell, which seemed much wider than normal. In the many years he'd occupied it, he'd measured the pit's width and walked its perimeter millions of times, but now he felt no boundaries. They weren't in a cell at all but in some limitless space.

Hasdiel led him to a soft, cushioned spot that had certainly never been there before, and he sat beside her. He felt the warmth of her hip and thigh pressed against his. The human body she wore was as solid as his, although hers was created from light and his from darkness.

He gazed at their joined hands, hers translucent and his opaque, and felt the strength of her fingers gripping him. She was much stronger than he was. She could pull him up to the heights of heaven if she wished and that thought frightened him. In this place, he knew what to expect—every torture he deserved—but the pinnacle was a dizzying, mysterious place.

The angel leaned toward him, demanding his attention. "Don't look so worried. You've earned your freedom. This is a good thing."

"How? What have I done to earn it?"

"It's not your actions, but your state of mind. At last you've grasped the concept of right and wrong and have repentance in your heart. For that alone you've earned a blessing."

"Absolution?"

She moved closer still, filling his vision with her ethereal countenance. "You were always forgiven but had to learn to begin to forgive yourself."

For violence, destruction and a life entirely devoid of kindness, he wasn't so certain he *had* done sufficient penance yet. But she was right in saying he saw the error of his ways now. That must count for something, or she wouldn't be here telling him there was a glimmer of hope at the end of the long, dark tunnel of his existence.

Hasdiel cradled his cheek in her hand and her breath brushed his mouth like feathers as she whispered, "I see the light in you and I will help you to bring it forth." Then she touched her lips to his in a gentle kiss.

He remembered flower petals, how they'd once been soft against his nose and smelled so sweet. Roses. A sun-drenched garden. How long since he'd thought of such a place? Something stirred within him and unfurled like a young plant growing toward the sun. He reached for the female form beside him and clung to her like a thorny vine clings to the rose that sustains it.

The woman was solid in his arms, not a creature of light as she appeared. She tasted like ripe apples fresh from a tree on a late September day. He remembered that taste and climbing trees, the bark scraping his palms, branches catching on his clothes. There had been good times, precious moments when he was young before he'd allowed his purer self to be buried under layers of filth.

The angel pulled away from his hungry mouth and smiled at him. "Do you see? All is not lost."

"But I ruined lives," he muttered. "I did unforgivable things."

"And you have paid a thousand times over for those sins. You have wallowed in guilt for centuries in this prison."

Micah didn't question her again about why she would give

such a worthless creature as him a moment of her time. It must be part of her job; take up a dirty rug and beat the dust out of it. He stopped questioning and reached for her again, letting her flow into his arms and fill them.

For right now, she was simply a beautiful woman and he, a lonely man. These were the roles they played. Her ephemeral gown evaporated and her firm flesh was soft and fragrant beneath his hands. He kissed the curve of her shoulder and wrapped his hands around her waist. The fullness of her breasts beckoned him, reminding him of other breasts he'd suckled and skin he'd touched. Her feminine body reminded him of long, black hair that smelled of oil and spices, women from his past—a mother and a wife. He'd hurt both of them through his selfishness. It seemed the women in his mortal life had always been crying.

Micah frowned at the flash of memory but didn't pull away from Hasdiel. Her breasts filled his hands and mouth, succulent and as ripe as fruit on the bough. He closed his eyes and drank the nectar of energy flowing through her hardened nipples. He tasted the fullness of life, which filled and lifted him. He felt more buoyant, more full of joy than he'd ever thought possible. The angel was the wellspring from which all goodness flowed.

She was yielding and warm against his hard, dark form. His erection thrust toward her, seeking to bury itself in her blissful comfort. But Micah fell to his knees before her to worship first. He kissed her soft, taut belly and the crease between her torso and leg. He licked the insides of her thighs, tasting her skin. Then he nuzzled her folds and inhaled the mystery of her essence.

Angel she might be, but garbed in this cloak of humanity, Hasdiel was as prone to moan and shudder as any woman. She arched beneath his tongue as he probed her opening and sampled her juices. Micah teased her clitoris with the tip of his tongue and once more faded memories of his long-ago wife came to mind. They had been good together at first. He had tended to her needs this way. But time had changed him and he'd forgotten how to give.

Now, Hasdiel's fingers caught in his hair. She clasped his head and held him to her as she thrust her hips. "Good," she murmured.

Memories flooded him. He recalled the pleasure in being able to bring a woman joy rather than pain. He hadn't always marched through life as ruthlessly and destructively as a child kicking over anthills. Sometimes he had shown gentleness, restraint, thoughtfulness—and not only in lovemaking. Good and generous qualities still lingered inside him. They blossomed now. He longed to please this angel in every way and bring her rapture.

Micah concentrated on his task, gripping her thighs and lapping until she writhed beneath him and cried out. Her voice was a temple gong, unearthly and reverberating, and her climax was more than a mortal orgasm. Tides changed course and the constellations whirled in space as Hasdiel came. He watched her beautiful face and stars sparkled in her eyes.

When her tremors died away, she rewarded him with a smile. "How sweetly you give of yourself. Now come into me and we will complete the union. You shall be fully healed."

He scrambled to his feet, too eager, stumbling and falling beside her on the soft bed she'd created for them to lie on. She laughed and held out her arms to him.

Micah crawled over her. He'd forgotten how it felt to rest between a woman's legs, her arms wrapped around him, her softness cushioning his body. Hasdiel's hands slid down his back and cupped his rear. She shifted and sighed beneath him.

How long did they remain that way—locked together in a warm embrace? It might have been seconds or years in this

place where time was not measured. Something loosened within
Micah, a knot untying, a cord snapping, and he felt he would
weep at the sheer pleasure of being held in her arms. The bliss of
emotion didn't diminish the hunger of his cock, however, which
swelled even harder and bumped against her entrance.

Micah pushed into his angel. He forged inside her. His
cockhead was surrounded by silken heat and he gasped at the
intensity. In that moment of entry, he remembered what home
had once meant; a fire on the hearth, a bowl full of hot food,
a welcoming woman to take his wet coat and tell him to dry
himself by the fire. He'd walked away from all of those incred-
ible things because of his own reckless nature. He'd chosen
dangerous pleasures, desired useless objects it took murder to
achieve, and his foolish longings had brought him so low that
he couldn't find his way out of the pit he'd dug.

Hot tears slipped from the corners of Micah's closed eyes as
he pushed deeply into the light of Hasdiel's body. Beyond the
joining of their two mortal forms, this was a spiritual union.
His soul was stripped bare and couldn't hide his worst secrets
from her. This angel knew all about him yet gave him uncondi-
tional love—such inconceivable generosity.

"Look at me," she murmured.

He obeyed, peering into her luminous eyes and seeing a
reflection of himself that wasn't horrifying or shameful. Her
gaze awakened his soul to its true nature, reminding him of
its purity. Past evil actions couldn't alter the gold beneath the
mud.

Micah slowly withdrew his cock and then thrust again. She
pulled him deeper, wrapped her arms and legs around him
tighter. They pushed against each other in a rhythm as strong
and steady as the flow of the universe. He filled her completely,
felt their bodies merge and become one and was transported.

He rose from his body and from the darkness of the cell. The universe around him expanded, layer upon layer, physical and astral planes coexisting. The entire cosmos was displayed before him and he was one with the angels. Not only the beautiful being whose temporary body surrounded his, but all of the shining spirits. Ecstasy flooded him. *We are one,* he marveled.

"We are one," the angel assured him as he came back to his mortal frame and her arms holding him.

Micah clung to her warmth and breathed in the floral scent of her body. He saw now that this savior was his natural counterpart, the positive force to balance his negative. Together they made a perfect whole and they were together at last. She had come to take him to his true home.

Micah was no longer in his tiny cell. The darkness of the pit was gone, blown away by his realization. Limitless space surrounded him and Hasdiel, fresh air, light and colors, but of a finer vibration than the gross physical world. It was almost too much beauty to take in for eyes that had seen nothing but blackness for so long. Celestial music flowed through him and lit him from within and Micah realized the body he'd clung to was unnecessary.

Hasdiel released him and rose, leaving her physical body behind like a dress that had grown too small. In her natural form, a being of untainted light, she was even more breathtaking. She reached out to Micah. "Are you ready now?"

"Yes. I am."

She took hold of him and drew him from his body. The last vestiges of the dark prison fell away and they rose together to supreme heights.

ABOUT THE
AUTHORS

KELLEY ARMSTRONG (KelleyArmstrong.com) is the author of the *New York Times* bestselling *Women of the Otherworld* series, which began with *Bitten*. She grew up in Southwestern Ontario, where she still lives with her family. A former computer programmer, she's now escaped her corporate cubicle and hopes never to return.

JANINE ASHBLESS (janineashbless.blogspot.com) is the author of five Black Lace books of fantasy and paranormal erotica. Her short stories have been published by Spice, Black Lace, Nexus, Xcite, Seal, Ellora's Cave and Cleis (including *Best Women's Erotica 2011* and *Best Bondage Erotica 2011*). She lives in England.

SHARON BIDWELL (sharonbidwell.co.uk) was born in London on New Year's Eve. Sharon's growing repertoire features twisted tales, cross-genre writing, critically acclaimed "deeply passionate" erotic romances, and vivid, unexpected, sometimes intensely magical worlds.

CLAIRE BUCKINGHAM is an aspiring novelist living in the deep south of New Zealand. Despite her sensible day job as a pharmacist, her writing's firmly in the paranormal and fantasy genres—and that's just the way she likes it.

ELIZABETH DANIELS's (elizabethdaniels.com) short erotic fiction has appeared in the ERWA anthology *CREAM*, *Best Bondage Erotica 2011* and *Gotta Have It: 69 Stories of Sudden Sex*. Elizabeth currently lives in Texas.

At childhood sleepovers, Michigan native **BONNIE DEE** was the designated ghost tale teller, thrilling listeners with macabre tales. A lifetime of writing followed. She most enjoys writing about damaged people who find healing with another soul. See her backlist of books at bonniedee.com.

ROSE DE FER sees the sensual in the strange, and she loves the view from the edge. She lives in England with her husband, who feeds her wine and raw meat and keeps the chains tight when the moon is full.

TAHIRA IQBAL is a UK-based writer who developed a love for writing when life got challenging and she needed an outlet to thrash out emotions that she couldn't articulate. For the last nine years, Tahira has worked in the film and TV industry. You can find her at tahiraiqbal.com.

ASHLEY LISTER (ashleylister.co.uk) is the pseudonymous author of more than two dozen erotic fiction titles and countless short stories, as well as two nonfiction titles exploring the secret lives of the United Kingdom's swinging community. Aside from working as a performance poet, he currently teaches creative writing in northwest England.

ANNA MEADOWS (meadowstories.blogspot.com) is a part-time executive assistant, part-time lesbian housewife. Her work appears in *Best Lesbian Romance 2010*, *Best Lesbian Romance 2011*, *Girls Who Bite* and on the Lambda Literary website. She lives and writes in Northern California.

EVAN MORA'S tales of love, lust and other demons have appeared in many fine publications including: *Best Lesbian Erotica 2009*, *Best Lesbian Romance 2009* and *2010*, *The Sweetest Kiss: Ravishing Vampire Erotica*, *Best Bondage Erotica 2011*, and *Gotta Have It: 69 Stories of Sudden Sex*. She lives in Toronto.

Eroticist **GISELLE RENARDE** (wix.com/gisellerenarde/erotica) is a queer Canadian, contributor to dozens of short-story anthologies, an avid volunteer, and author of numerous electronic and print books. Ms. Renarde lives across from a park with two bilingual cats that sleep on her head.

CHARLOTTE STEIN (themightycharlottestein.blogspot.com) has published many stories in various anthologies, including *Fairy Tale Lust*. Her own collection of shorts was named one of the best erotic romances of 2009 by Michelle Buonfiglio. She also has novellas out with Ellora's Cave, Total-E-Bound and Xcite. She lives in West Yorkshire, England.

ZANDER VYNE (zandervyne.com) is published in hundreds of books featuring pretentious author's bios. There won't be any of that here. Dislikes: mad cow disease, warm beer. Likes: secondhand bookstores, traveling. Miscellanea: lived on a sailboat for seven years, sang in a rock band. Zander currently lives in Chicago.

CARRIE WILLIAMS's work includes novels *The Blue Guide*, *Chilli Heat* and *The Apprentice*. Her vampire erotica story "The Man Eaters" made *The Mammoth Book of Best New Erotica 9*. Also a travel journalist, Carrie's usually on the road but can often be found in London, Manchester or Paris.

ABOUT
THE EDITOR

MITZI SZERETO is an author and anthology editor of erotic and multi-genre fiction and nonfiction. She has her own blog, Errant Ramblings: Mitzi Szereto's Weblog (mitziszereto.com/blog), and a Web TV channel, Mitzi TV (mitziszereto.com/tv), which covers the "quirky" side of London. Her books include *Pride and Prejudice: Hidden Lusts*; *In Sleeping Beauty's Bed: Erotic Fairy Tales*; *Getting Even: Revenge Stories*; *The New Black Lace Book of Women's Sexual Fantasies*; *Wicked: Sexy Tales of Legendary Lovers*; *Dying for It: Tales of Sex and Death* and the *Erotic Travel Tales* anthologies. A popular social media personality and frequent interviewee, she has pioneered erotic writing workshops in the United Kingdom and Europe and has lectured in creative writing at several British universities. Originally from the United States, she lives in Greater London. Exercise extreme caution if approaching on the night of a full moon. (Or if she's within biting range of Ian Somerhalder.)